Prologue

Excerpt from the Book of Frostfire, Solariate Canon – Verse of the Silent Heir

He shall be born beneath the breathless storm.
His name will vanish from fire and be etched into ice.
The child of silence, the Coldborn Flame.

He shall not beg for the crown, nor hunger for the sword.
But the world will bend all the same.
And the stars will call him Ith'Kaladrin.

Not to save us.
To end what we became.

Chapter 1: The Breath Before Snowfall

The bells rang early in the morning.

Three deep chimes echoed through the freezing air, slow and mournful, like the bones of some old-world groaning beneath the weight of another endless winter.

I stood by my bedroom window with my arms crossed, trying to stay warm. The thick stone walls of the castle didn't help much. Outside, the sky over Erythra looked like a fading bruise—gray, cold, and tired. Snow was already falling, light and steady, the kind that never really stopped. Here, the snow was less a season and more a truth.

Down below, soldiers moved across the courtyard. They trained, marched, swapped guard duties with a rhythm so practiced it seemed mechanical. These were the Winter Blades, my father's elite. He believed discipline should start before the sun even rose. I figured he thought the same applied to me.

My room was quiet. The soft buzz of the wall heaters and the faint hiss of the kettle were the only sounds. I hadn't touched the tea left for me. Servants came and went without speaking. I didn't know their names, and they didn't expect mine. To them, I was just the second son of Thalos Valerius—not the heir, just the other one. A background figure in a house too cold to notice its own shadows.

My sister, Cersei, would already be at the war council. She never missed one.

Not because she needed to impress our father. Because she was made for leadership.

And me? I was made to survive.

I turned from the window and dressed slowly, layering the heavy, formal clothing expected of my bloodline. Black fabric lined with silver thread, the crest of our house—an ice-crowned wolf—sewn into the collar.

I wore it because I had to. Not because I cared.

The halls of the citadel were colder than the air outside. Frost bit into the seams where stone met steel. Torches burned blue with chemical flame, flickering low in the drafty corridors.

Most mornings, the halls were empty except for the occasional murmured footsteps of scholars, servants, or guards. People here moved like they were trying not to be noticed. Like they knew the walls remembered everything.

Except Elias.

He sat outside the solar atrium, where the clergy kept the old texts and Frostfire relics. His robes were simple—gray and white, worn at the edges. A polished cane rested across his knees, but he never seemed to need it.

"You're up early today, my prince," he said without turning.

"I didn't sleep," I replied.

He nodded, as if that made all the sense in the world.

"It feels colder," I said after a moment.

"The sky is preparing to grieve."

I glanced sideways at him. "Is that from scripture?"

A faint smile tugged at the corner of his mouth. "No. Just something I remember."

I lingered longer than I meant to. Elias had a way of making the cold quieter somehow. Less hostile.

As I turned to leave, he spoke again—softly, like the words were meant to slip past the frost.

"The Solariate has eyes beyond Erythra. You know that don't you?"

"I know."

"They're watching your family again. Closely."

I didn't answer.

"They're whispering names in the dark," Elias continued, voice low. "Old names. Dangerous ones."

I let the silence grow thick between us before I finally said, "They've always whispered."

Elias looked up, his gaze pale and steady. "Maybe so. But never this loud."

His words followed me like frost clinging to the hem of a cloak.

The throne hall was cavernous and cold; more tomb than throne. Tall black pillars lined the way to the seat at the far end—a monolithic block of carved stone, set against windows rimed in frost.

My father sat there, unmoving.

King Thalos Valerius didn't need to speak to be feared. He only had to exist.

He watched me cross the vast floor. His gaze was heavy, not with anger or pride— just a hard, impersonal judgment that had weighed on me since childhood.

"You weren't at council," he said. Not a question. A fact.

I bowed slightly, the barest movement. "Cersei attended."

"I called for you."

Not her. You.

I said nothing.

He motioned to the empty space beside his throne. "You'll be there at the next meeting. No excuses."

"Yes, Father."

The silence between us was not uncomfortable. It was normal. Expected.

He turned his head slightly, studying the frost gathering at the corners of the windows. "The storm grows worse. War is near. You must become more than a symbol."

The words hit harder than any shout.

More than a symbol.

I kept my expression neutral. Gave a nod. Turned and left without another word.

Later that day, I found myself on the high balcony overlooking the capital. The wind knifed through the mountains, howling past towers and frozen spires, but I barely felt it anymore.

From up here, the people were small gray shapes drifting through streets carved into the snow. They moved with purpose but not hope.

To them, I wasn't a prince.

I wasn't a threat.

I wasn't anything.

Just a name sewn into banners they barely bothered to look at anymore.

I was still watching when the banners of House Marcerin entered the gates.

Silver and ash.

Lucien had returned.

And with him, the first sign that everything was about to change.

Chapter 2: The White Market

The bells still echoed faintly through the stone corridors by the time I left the upper floors of the citadel behind.

I pulled my heavy coat tighter around me as I moved through the inner halls. Even inside, frost grew in the corners like veins under pale skin. The citadel had been built to withstand sieges and winters that could last entire years. Comfort had never been part of its design.

Most mornings, the halls were nearly empty, but today the servants moved faster, their steps sharper. Word of Lucien Marcerin's arrival traveled ahead of him like a weather front. Everyone knew why he had come.

An alliance.

Or something worse.

I found myself moving toward the lower levels without thinking. Toward the White Market.

The market wasn't officially part of the citadel. It was the network of underground streets and courtyards tucked between the ancient foundations, half-forgotten by the architects but reclaimed by merchants, smiths, and traders over centuries. Here, under the heavy frost and heavy eyes of the nobility, the real heart of the city beat—quiet, desperate, stubborn.

The White Market earned its name honestly. Ice slicked the stones year-round, and even the iron lanterns overhead wore coats of frost.

I tightened my gloves and moved through the early crowd. Stalls lined the narrow paths; their keepers bundled in thick furs. They hawked weapons, books, frozen herbs, even relics stolen from forgotten Solariate shrines. Nobody asked where the goods came from. As long as coin traded hands, no one cared.

A few merchants nodded respectfully as I passed, but most avoided eye contact. The Valerius crest on my coat might as well have been a brand.

I didn't blame them.

They had no reason to trust royalty anymore.

At the far end of the market, near the broken aqueducts where the frost ran thickest, I spotted him.

Lucien Marcerin stood like he owned the place.

He wore his House's colors: silver and ash, stitched into a heavy traveling cloak. His hair was dark, his posture relaxed, but there was a stillness to him, like a blade waiting to be drawn.

He turned when he sensed me and smiled easily. "Noctis."

I approached slowly. "You made good time."

"Good roads," he said, glancing around the market. "And better horses."

His eyes flicked over the merchants, the crumbling stone, the layers of snow that even the fires couldn't fully melt.

"This place hasn't changed," he said.

"It never does," I said.

Lucien laughed softly, but there was something else in it. Not mockery exactly—something colder. Calculating.

We stood there for a moment, two princes of dying houses pretending we were still part of something permanent.

"You're early," I said.

"I like to see the bones of a city before I meet its rulers," Lucien said. "Tells you what matters."

"And what do Erythra's bones tell you?"

He smiled wider. "They tell me you're running out of time."

I stiffened slightly. "You came for an alliance. Not insults."

"I came to see if there's still anything left to ally with," he said simply.

The words hit harder than I let him see.

Lucien wasn't just here for politics. He was here to measure the rot.

Before I could answer, a familiar voice cut through the thin air.

"Noctis."

I turned.

Cersei approached across the frost-slick stones, her coat whipping behind her like a banner. She wore no crown, but she carried herself like she did. She moved with absolute purpose, a quiet storm in human shape.

Lucien straightened slightly, his smile thinning. Even he knew better than to underestimate her.

"Sister," I said.

She nodded to me, then to Lucien—politely, but without warmth.

"We're needed," she said simply.

Lucien arched a brow. "Already?"

Cersei didn't answer him. Her eyes remained on me, steady, unreadable.

I followed her without a word.

As we moved through the twisting market paths, she finally spoke—quietly, so only I could hear.

"Be careful with him," she said.

"I know," I replied.

"No," she said, voice colder now. "You think you know. Lucien Marcerin isn't here just for treaties. He's here because he smells blood."

I glanced at her sharply.

"And if he doesn't find enough of it," she continued, "he'll make more."

We walked in silence after that, the frost crunching under our boots, the banners overhead creaking in the wind.

The climb back up to the citadel was steep, lined with ancient statues whose faces had long been erased by ice and time. Watching. Waiting.

At the threshold of the upper halls, Cersei paused.

"You shouldn't have gone down there alone," she said without looking at me.

"I wasn't exactly alone," I said.

"Lucien isn't company," she snapped, low and sharp. "He's a knife looking for a sheath."

I smirked. "Maybe we're all knives."

Cersei finally looked at me, her eyes narrowing—not with anger, but with something more dangerous.

"Learn the difference," she said. "Before he teaches it to you."

Then she turned and disappeared into the upper halls, her footsteps silent on the frostbitten stone.

I stood there a moment longer, feeling the weight of her words settle into the cold air around me.

Above the distant roofs of the capital, black banners stirred in the rising wind.

The world was changing.

And soon, blood would stain the snow.

Chapter 3: The Proposal

The council chamber was where we waited

Frost traced the old banners hanging from the stone columns. The light filtering through the stained glass was pale and sickly, casting broken colors over the council table where the high lords and envoys sat waiting.

At the head of the room, the throne rose like a black monolith. King Thalos Valerius sat upon it, silent, his expression carved from the same stone as the walls.

Cersei stood to his right.

I stood to his left.

We were mirrors of each other—opposite in almost every way except blood.

The doors at the far end groaned open, and the Marcerin delegation entered.

Lucien led them, flanked by his father's advisors. He walked like he owned the room, every step measured, every glance calculated. Behind him, banners of House Marcerin unfurled: silver crossed with ash.

They bowed with precision, more out of formality than respect.

King Thalos didn't move.

Lucien's second, a tall man with hair like wet iron, stepped forward and spoke.

"In the name of House Marcerin," he said, voice carrying easily, "we offer terms of alliance, loyalty, and blood. We recognize the strength of House Valerius and wish to bind our fates together—so no storm, no famine, no war may ever divide us."

He turned slightly, gesturing to Lucien.

"My lord proposes union with Lady Cersei Valerius."

Silence fell over the hall like a shroud.

The offer wasn't unexpected.

But hearing it aloud made something tighten in my chest.

Cersei didn't flinch. She stepped forward, every inch the daughter of kings.

"My lord," she said, voice clear and cold, "I recognize the honor your House extends. But House Valerius is not in need of saviors. We are not yet fallen."

Lucien's eyes flickered—just for a moment.

His second pressed on. "It is not salvation we offer, but partnership. Strength joined to strength."

Cersei tilted her head slightly, studying him like a sword studying a scabbard. "And yet, somehow, your House stands to gain much more than ours."

A few nervous chuckles rippled through the minor nobles. Quickly silenced.

King Thalos finally spoke, his voice low but resonant.

"Our House has endured for generations without aid," he said. "We will endure without chains disguised as favors."

It wasn't anger.

It was certainty.

Lucien stepped forward himself now, hands open in a gesture of peace.

"No chains," he said. "Only a future where neither of our peoples have to starve or bleed alone."

He looked at Cersei when he said it.

Not me.

Not the king.

Cersei didn't look away. "If the price of survival is submission, we will freeze before we kneel."

The temperature in the hall seemed to drop another degree.

King Thalos rose from his throne—not quickly, but with the inevitable gravity of a mountain shifting.

The Marcerin delegation stepped back instinctively.

"You have our answer," Thalos said. His gaze pinned Lucien where he stood. "There will be no union."

Lucien bowed slightly, masking whatever thoughts moved behind his cool exterior.

"As you wish," he said.

The delegation turned and withdrew, their banners trailing like wounded shadows behind them.

When the doors slammed shut again, the tension remained.

Thalos didn't sit back down.

Instead, he turned to face us.

"You have made an enemy," he said.

Cersei bowed her head slightly. "Better an enemy we chose than an ally who would have strangled us in our sleep."

Thalos looked at me, then at her.

"For now," he said. "Prepare yourselves. The Marcerin's are not fools. They will not forget this insult."

Then he left the hall, his cloak trailing frost in his wake.

Cersei remained still for a long moment.

So, did I.

It was Cersei who finally broke the silence.

"They were never here for peace," she said quietly.

"I know," I said.

But part of me—some small, stupid part—had wanted to believe it could be different.

That maybe not every path forward had to be soaked in blood.

I looked at the stained glass again.

The colors seemed even duller now.

Chapter 4: The Silence of Kings

The throne room was colder than the halls, colder even than the White Market.

Frost climbed the high pillars like grasping hands. Light filtered weakly through the rime-caked windows, painting the black stone floor in broken, colorless shards.

I stood before the throne.

Cersei stood beside me.

King Thalos sat like a monument atop the black seat of House Valerius; the wolf-crest of our bloodline carved into the stone at his back. His cloak hung heavy around him; more ice than fabric now.

He studied us both with the same hard, measuring gaze he'd carried since Selene died.

"You acted without consulting me," he said, voice low but carrying through the empty hall.

Cersei didn't flinch. "There was no time."

"There is always time," Thalos said. "Time to weigh, to measure. To know the cost."

"The cost of bending to House Marcerin would have been steeper," she replied.

He leaned forward slightly, the frost creaking under his movement.

"And yet now we must prepare for war," he said. "You made that choice for all of us."

"I made the choice you would have made," Cersei said.

A beat of silence.

His gaze shifted to me.

"And you," he said. "Where do you stand, Noctis?"

The question cut deeper than any sword.

Not because I didn't know the answer.

But because I did.

"I stand with my family," I said quietly.

Something flickered across Thalos's face. Not approval. Not pride.

Something colder.

Resignation.

For a moment, the weight of the hall, the weight of the coming war, the weight of every cold day that had ever pressed down on Erythra pressed against my chest.

And I remembered a day when the halls had been warm.

When the cold hadn't yet won.

When I had still believed the world could be different.

I was younger then. Maybe six or seven.

The sun had been out that day—a rare, golden thing over the white streets of Erythra's capital.

My mother, Selene, had taken us—Cersei and me—down from the citadel into the city proper. No banners, no armed procession. Just family.

Thalos had come too, though he wore no crown that day. Just a heavy dark coat, his face less grim, his steps lighter.

I remembered the sound of the city: music playing from the White Market, children laughing as they chased each other across the frost-worn stones. Merchants called out their wares—jewels that caught the sunlight like fire, fabrics dyed every shade of dusk and dawn.

The people flocked to my mother.

They reached for her hand—not to drag her down, but to touch a piece of something they thought had been lost. She smiled at them without fear. Without arrogance.

She knelt to bless a newborn swaddled in a worn blanket. Whispered something to an old woman bent double with age. Bought a bright red ribbon from a little girl's stall and tied it into my hair while I protested, laughing.

Cersei laughed too—unburdened, unguarded.

Even Thalos smiled, faintly, as he watched us.

The city had loved Selene.

We all had.

Even then, though I hadn't understood it, I had seen the strain beneath her beauty. The way she leaned a little heavier on Thalos's arm when she thought no one was looking. The way her hands trembled sometimes when she thought no one would notice.

But she never showed weakness to the people.

Not once.

She walked among them like a queen of life, not of death.

And they adored her for it.

I remembered the way the sun caught her hair, making it shine like a crown woven from starlight.

I remembered thinking she would never leave us.

That she was too strong.

Too bright.

I had been wrong.

The cold of the present snapped back into me like a blade.

I blinked and the memory burned away into the frost and the broken light of the throne room.

King Thalos was still watching me.

"Family is not a shield," he said quietly. "It is a weight. One you will either carry—or be crushed by."

He rose slowly, the sound of his cloak dragging over the stone like the whisper of an executioner's blade.

"We will prepare for what comes," he said. "There will be no more mistakes."

He left the hall without another word, his steps echoing in the emptiness he left behind.

Cersei stood rigid beside me; her jaw tight.

For a long moment, neither of us moved.

Finally, she spoke, her voice so low I almost didn't hear it.

"I won't let us fall," she said.

I didn't answer.

I wasn't sure if I believed her.

Not because I doubted her strength.

But because I had seen how even the brightest lights could flicker and die.

And how no one—not even kings or queens—could stop the cold from coming.

Chapter 5: The Weight of Steel

The council chamber buzzed with quiet tension.

Maps littered the black stone table. Pins marked border towns, strongholds, river crossings. Everywhere I looked, the same grim pattern formed: House Marcerin tightening its grip, circling us like wolves around a wounded elk.

Cersei stood at the head of the table, hands clasped behind her back, sharp-eyed and unreadable.

"Our scouts report increased Marcerin activity along the southern ridges," one of the advisors said, his voice tight. "Small encampments. Supply lines being fortified."

"They're preparing for a siege," another muttered.

"No," Cersei said, silencing the murmurs with a single word. "Not a siege. Not yet. They're testing us. Probing our defenses. Looking for cracks."

I watched her work, admired the calm, precise way she broke apart their movements with surgical clarity. She wasn't just born for command. She had become it, shaped by necessity, by the slow death of everything we once were.

"We should move preemptively," someone suggested.

"And stretch our forces thin?" Cersei's gaze cut him down where he stood. "No. We fortify key positions. We wait."

"And if they strike first?" the advisor pressed.

Cersei smiled—cold and without humor. "Then we bleed them on our terms, not theirs."

Around the table, heads nodded reluctantly. Even here, even now, they recognized the fire inside her.

I should have felt reassured.

Instead, all I felt was the slow tightening of a noose around our throats.

The meeting adjourned. The advisors filed out in twos and threes, whispering among themselves.

Cersei lingered only long enough to glance at me. "You should be training," *she said quietly.* "You're not ready."

I wanted to argue.

But she was right.

And there was only one person in the citadel who could make me ready fast enough.

The training grounds behind the citadel were older than the palace itself—worn by centuries of frost and war drills. The air smelled of iron, oil, and frozen sweat.

Commander Ysra waited for me near the sparring rings; her posture relaxed but alert. She wore simple training armor—gray leather reinforced with strips of black iron. No rank, no medals. Just a soldier ready to break me down and build me back up.

"Late," *she said as I approached.*

"Council ran long," *I muttered.*

"Excuses run longer," *she replied, tossing me a blunted training sword.* "Draw."

I caught it awkwardly, the weight unfamiliar in my hands.

Ysra circled me slowly, appraising my stance with a predator's eye. "You've trained with court tutors, I assume?"

I nodded.

"Forget everything they taught you."

Before I could respond, she lunged.

The world snapped into focus.

I barely managed to parry, the force of her blow jolting up my arms.

Again.
And again.

Ysra pressed me hard, every strike measured, testing. I stumbled, regained footing, lost it again.

"You're thinking too much," she barked. "Fighting isn't about memory. It's about instinct."

I gritted my teeth and lunged forward, trying to catch her off balance.

She sidestepped effortlessly, knocking the blade from my hands with a flick of her wrist.

I went down hard, the frozen earth knocking the breath from my lungs.

Ysra stood over me, not gloating—just waiting.

"Again," she said.

I pushed up, grabbed the sword, and faced her.

We went on like that for what felt like hours. Strike. Counter. Fall. Rise.

Somewhere in the chaos of it, something shifted.

Time seemed to slow—not in the literal sense, not yet—but enough that I saw her next move before it came. My body moved before my mind caught up. A clean block. A counterstrike that forced Ysra back a half-step.

Her eyes narrowed slightly.

"Good," she said. "Again."

I didn't know what had changed.

Only that it was there.

Beneath my skin.

Waiting.

Watching.

Later, bruised and half-frozen, I made my way back into the citadel.

The corridors seemed darker somehow, the frost thicker on the walls. Maybe it was just the exhaustion—or maybe the weight of what was coming finally settling into my bones.

Cersei met me outside the smaller council chamber. She wore her training leathers too, but there was no sweat on her brow, no signs of fatigue. Only focus.

"Father's waiting," she said simply.

We entered together.

King Thalos stood at the far end of the room, staring out a frost-smeared window at the dead city beyond.

He didn't turn when we approached.

"Reports confirm what we feared," he said. "Marcerin forces mass at the borders. They're waiting for us to make the first mistake."

"We won't," Cersei said firmly.

Thalos finally faced us. His expression was heavier than the crown he wore.

"Readiness is not certainty," he said. "And certainty is not survival."

He stepped toward us, each movement deliberate, as if even standing had become a battle.

"You will be tested," he said, voice low. "Not just by them. By your own blood. By your own oaths."

Neither of us spoke.

He studied us both for a long moment before finally speaking again.

"There is rot beneath the snow," he said. "It festers in the cracks of loyalty and pride. If we are to survive, you must be willing to cut it out—no matter how deep."

The room seemed to shrink around us, the cold pressing harder against my skin.

I swallowed, forcing the words out. "We understand."

Thalos's gaze lingered on me longer than necessary.

"I wonder," he said softly.

He turned away, the conversation clearly over.

We left in silence.

Only when we were alone in the hallway did I realize my hands were shaking—not from fear. From something else.

A whisper stirred at the edge of my mind.

Cut it out... no matter how deep.

I clenched my fists until the cold bit deep into my skin, trying to banish the voice.

But it was no longer something I could ignore.

It was growing.

It was waiting.

And soon, it would no longer ask politely for my attention.

Chapter 6: Shadows Between Walls

First Light in the Frost

The bells echoed faintly through the citadel, the sound barely touching the frost-heavy corridors. Outside the narrow windows, the sky remained an endless stretch of pale gray, offering no warmth, no comfort.

I stood in the cloister near the old chapel, arms crossed against the cold, watching the snow gather in the cracks of the ancient stone. The city beyond the citadel walls looked smaller every day, buried deeper under the endless weight of winter and fear.

Elias was there too, leaning lightly on his cane, his gaze distant but sharp beneath the folds of his hood.

"You feel it," he said quietly.

I didn't answer right away.

"The way the world holds its breath before the breaking point," he continued. "As if even the stones know what's coming."

I shifted my stance, the cold biting through the thick layers of my coat. "The Marcerin's?"

"And others," Elias said, his voice low, almost a whisper. "When one wall crumbles, it is not just one enemy who walks through the breach."

I glanced sideways at him. "You think we have more enemies inside the walls than outside?"

Elias smiled faintly. Not amused—just resigned.

"I think survival breeds strange loyalties," he said. "And fear can be as sharp as any blade."

For a moment, the only sound was the wind scraping against the stone arches.

"They expect too much," I said quietly. "Cersei. My father. The council. They expect me to be something I'm not."

"They expect you to become what you must," Elias corrected gently. "Not for them. For the people who cannot carry their own burdens."

I looked out at the city again, feeling its weight press into me.

"You are not alone, Noctis," Elias said, voice softer now. "Even when it feels that way."

He tapped his cane against the stone once—an old, rhythmic gesture—and then he turned, disappearing into the deep shadowed halls without another word.

I wasn't left to my thoughts for long.

A page found me a few minutes later—a boy no older than twelve, breathless from running the icy corridors.

"Prince Noctis," he stammered, bowing hastily. "Commander Ysra requests your presence in the south training hall."

I nodded, feeling a small pulse of unease. Ysra wasn't someone who summoned lightly.

The walk to the training hall was brisk. My boots echoed sharply against the stones, the cold gnawing deeper the further down into the bowels of the citadel I went.

The hall was brightly lit by chemical torches that burned cold blue against the frost-lined walls. Commander Ysra stood near the center, her arms folded behind her back, her posture rigid even at rest.

Beside her stood several soldiers—new faces, clad in the charcoal and silver of House Valerius's elite guard. Their armor was polished but practical, designed for survival rather than ceremony.

One among them caught my attention immediately.

She stood a little apart from the others, not in arrogance, but in a quiet, grounded way. Her hair was bound tightly behind her head, her stance balanced and alert. Everything about her spoke of training—not ostentation, not ambition. Just readiness.

"This," Ysra said without preamble, "is your new personal guard assignment."

She gestured briefly toward the small group.

"The escalation at the borders demands tighter security protocols," she continued. "Only those I trust completely are being assigned to direct protection details."

Her tone made it clear that trust was a rare commodity.

She motioned toward the woman who had drawn my attention.

"Lyra was handpicked by me," Ysra said. "Quiet. Disciplined. Efficient."

Lyra stepped forward smoothly and bowed, her movements sharp and without hesitation.

"Your Highness," she said, her voice steady, clear, professional.

There was no deference in her tone—only respect. No attempt to flatter, no fear. Just the quiet certainty of someone who knew exactly who she was.

I found myself studying her without meaning to—the way she carried herself, the way she seemed to blend into the space around her without disappearing.

"You trained under Ysra directly?" I asked, keeping my voice formal.

"Yes, Your Highness," Lyra answered without embellishment.

Ysra nodded curtly. "She's survived five live exercises that most veterans failed. She follows orders. And she thinks on her feet."

I let my gaze linger a moment longer before nodding once.

"Very well," I said. *"I look forward to seeing that discipline firsthand."*

A flicker of something—almost amusement, but too brief to catch properly—passed through Lyra's eyes.

She bowed again, then stepped back into line with the others.

Ysra dismissed the guards shortly after, her instructions sharp and final.

As Lyra filed out with the rest, she didn't glance back.

Neither did I.

But a part of me knew—without knowing why—that this was not the last time our paths would cross in ways neither of us could yet understand.

The frost grew thicker on the windows as I turned to leave, the wind howling low against the citadel walls.

Another whisper stirred at the edges of my mind—soft, waiting.

Change was coming.

And some things, once set in motion, could never be undone.

Chapter 7: Beneath the Mountain

The air was thinner beneath the mountain.

The inner training yard sat carved into the base of Erythra's oldest peak, surrounded on all sides by walls of black stone and ice-veined steel. A dome of faint light shimmered above the space, filtering what little sun reached this far down.

Commander Ysra stood at the edge of the ring, arms crossed, watching me bleed.

"Again," she said.

I picked up the blade.

My breath burned in my throat, and my ribs ached from where she had caught me with the blunt edge of a polearm. The other guards had long since stopped watching. This wasn't training.

It was reshaping.

We fought until I collapsed.

Not from injury—just everything else. Cold, exhaustion, doubt. It all hit at once. I dropped to one knee in the frostbitten dust, breathing like the mountain itself was pressing down on my chest.

Ysra knelt beside me, impassive.

"You're too careful," she said. "You fight like someone afraid to be cruel."

"Maybe I am."

"Then you're not ready," she said.

She stood, the frost crunching under her boots.

"But you're close."

Later, Lyra found me seated in the barracks medical wing.
She didn't speak at first. She simply took the cloth from my hands and started wrapping my arm herself.

"You missed a cut," she said, nodding at the thin slice running across my forearm.

"I thought I had," I muttered.

She didn't smile. Didn't mock. Just cleaned it. Bound it.

"I don't think she wants me to survive it," I said quietly.

"She doesn't care if you survive," Lyra replied. "She cares if you're ready."

"And if I'm not?"

Lyra looked up, meeting my eyes.
"Then she'll replace you. Before the world gets a chance to."

Her hands were steady, but her voice wasn't cold. Just honest.

I didn't speak after that.

But I didn't pull away, either.

The palace halls grew colder that week.

Not from temperature, but from tension. Every footstep echoed louder. Every glance from a servant carried something behind it—hope, or fear, or questions they didn't dare ask aloud.

I passed a pair of kitchen aides whispering near the gallery stairs.

"...he's the one, they're saying. The Frostborne, the—"

They fell silent as I passed.

But the words followed me anyway.

Elias stood at the top of the observatory tower, his robes swept by the wind. Across from him, a traveler in deep-blue armor knelt on one knee, dust from a long journey still clinging to his boots.

"The signs match," the traveler said. "Even the visions. The old texts..."

Elias said nothing, his gaze distant.

The traveler looked up. "You think it's him?"

"I think," Elias said quietly, "that the wind has returned to Erythra. And wind never comes without storm."

At the next council meeting, I sat beside Cersei.

She looked pale. Not tired—she would never allow herself that—but stretched thin, like a blade sharpened too many times.

She didn't ask how the training was going. She didn't ask if I had spoken to Elias, or if the rumors were bothering me.

She only passed me a data pad.

"Selari corridor's no longer theory," she said. "Marcerin ships moved past the line. They're cloaked, but we know."

"What's the response?"

"Nothing yet," she said. "We wait."

"Why?"

"Because Lucien wants us to move first."

I looked at her. "You're going to let him?"

She turned her eyes to mine. There was no anger there. Just steel.

"No," she said. "But I'm going to make sure when we do, there's no turning back."

That night, I couldn't sleep again.

Lyra stood her post as always, silent at the edge of the room. I didn't speak to her. Didn't need to.

The fire remained unlit. I didn't want warmth. I wanted quiet.

But something woke me.

A pressure.

Like gravity shifting the wrong way. Like a breath taken too deep.

The room was silent.

But frost had crept across the inside of the windows—jagged lines in patterns I didn't recognize. My breath hung in the air, suspended. Still.

And then, beneath it all, something else.

A voice.

Soft.

Precise.

Not my own.

"You are late."

I sat up, heart hammering against my ribs.

The frost on the glass began to melt, slow rivulets running down the jagged patterns.

The silence pressed closer, heavier, almost expectant.

The voice did not come again.

But something had shifted.

Something had woken.

And it was waiting.

Chapter 8: The Voice in the Ice

The frost hadn't melted.

Not completely.

By morning, the strange webwork on the windows had faded from sight—but not from memory. Thin veins of it clung to the corners, like something had reached for me and hadn't let go. I traced a fingertip across the glass and felt the faintest chill still lingering there, even as the palace warmed with the rising day.

Lyra stood outside my door, exactly where she'd been the night before. She looked at me—not with concern, but with a quiet evaluation. She knew something was off.

She didn't ask.

Neither did I.

I moved through the day with the shape of silence pressed against my skin.

In the war chamber, the ministers spoke with fraying confidence. The maps flickered with bright warnings. Names of outposts, coordinates of shadows. Whispers of unrest slipped between the official reports, thin as mist.

I sat in silence beside Cersei. Her expression was harder than usual—more statue than sister. She didn't speak to me. But I felt her watching me from time to time, the way a hawk might watch a wounded bird.

Not out of pity.

Out of strategy.

After the meeting, she passed me a data pad without looking at me. On it: confirmed fleet movements from Marcerin-controlled sectors. Cloaked, evasive, never direct. But too coordinated to be coincidence.

"They're waiting for us to make the first mistake," she said.

"And if we don't?"

"Then they'll escalate until they get the excuse."

I shifted the pad slightly, scanning the map again. "We should pressure their lines. Hit their supply chains before they entrench."

Cersei finally looked at me—sharp, cold.

"You think Lucien hasn't baited that move?"

I said nothing. She leaned in slightly, lowering her voice to a blade's edge.

"He wants us to bleed first. To look reckless."

"And if we hold?"

Her answer was colder still. "Then he'll find another reason to set the field on fire. With or without our help."

I nodded, feeling the weight settle deeper.

"So, what's our next move?" *I asked.*

"Preparation. Fortification. And if necessary... provocation."

Later that afternoon, I returned to the training yard beneath the mountain.

Ysra didn't say a word when I arrived. She simply handed me a practice blade heavier than any she'd given before. When I held it, the steel felt like gravity itself, dragging me downward.

Then she came at me.

No warning. No warm-up.

Her strikes weren't just fast—they were surgical, punishing.
She drove me backward with every blow, forcing me to rely on instinct, on desperation.

And just as I lunged—

The world broke.

I was somewhere else.

White ash floated through the air like snow, but the air was hot, dry, laced with copper. Before me stood a throne—not made of gold or obsidian, but something colder. Something crystalline. Almost like glass that had once been ice.

Around it, figures knelt in silence. Their faces were covered. Their weapons laid down at their sides.

Above us, the sky was fractured. A golden tear split the heavens, leaking light.

I reached for the blade at my hip—

And I was back.

Face down in the frost of the training yard, the taste of blood in my mouth, the cold ringing in my ears like a bell that wouldn't stop.

Ysra loomed over me. Her silhouette blurred against the cold light.

"What happened?" she demanded.

I didn't answer.

She stared for a long moment, her jaw tightening.

"Get up," she said finally. "Or don't. But don't come back until you choose."

There was no anger in her voice.

Only disappointment.

The kind you didn't get a second chance to fix.

Lyra found me hours later, sitting near one of the watch posts at the edge of the barracks wall.
I didn't hear her approach. She simply sat beside me, setting down a flask of water between us.

"You didn't report back," she said.

"I needed air."

"You needed to stand."

I didn't look at her. "How long have you been assigned to watch me?"

"A few days."

"And before that?"

"On rotation. I trained under Ysra. Like you."

"I doubt she ever threw you around like she does me."

"She did," Lyra said quietly. "Difference is, I stopped trying to prove something."

That stung more than I expected. I didn't respond.

She let the silence stretch, then said softer, almost an afterthought:

"Pain doesn't make you worthy, Noctis. Surviving it does."

I glanced sideways at her. The honesty in her voice was heavier than any lecture Ysra had ever given.

"You flinched today," she said. "In training. And not because you were afraid."

I finally turned toward her fully.
"I saw something," I said. "I don't know what. A place. A... moment. But it wasn't here."

She studied me, her brow furrowing slightly.

"You should tell Cersei," She said.

"She has enough to worry about."

Lyra didn't argue.

She just nodded once and stood.

"Then you'd better figure out what it means before someone else does."

And she left me sitting in the growing cold.

That evening, the palace buzzed with low murmurs—servants whispering in corners, lesser nobles exchanging half-glances in the galleries.
Word was spreading faster than orders could contain it.

The Frostborn Flame.

The Ith'Kaladrin.

I heard one of the kitchen aides whisper as I passed through the lower hall:
"It's him. Has to be. He walks where the snow won't fall."

I kept walking.

That night, I didn't light the hearth.
I didn't change out of the day's clothes.
I simply sat at the edge of my bed, staring at the windows.

And waiting.

The room darkened slowly.

Shadows stretched too far across the stone floor. The cold deepened—not biting, but deliberate, as if the room itself were holding its breath.

Then came the voice.

Not from the hall.
Not from behind me.
From within the silence.

"You were born in a storm."

I didn't move.

"She held you by the hearth. She said your name meant peace."

My throat tightened.

No one knew that. No one alive.

"You are not what they see. You are not what they want."

A pause. Almost like a smile in the darkness.

"But you are what's left."

The frost on the windows thickened again, blooming outward from invisible points.

*"You carry silence like a sword.
You dream of warmth but build kingdoms of ash."*

My breath caught in my chest.

The voice softened, almost kindly:

"I have been waiting for you, Noctis."

And then—

Silence.

Total.

Final.

Chapter 9: Echoes Beneath the Skin

The war council gathered before dawn.

The chamber lights were low, and the table was already glowing with tactical overlays—layered blueprints of Erythra's defenses and the expanding reach of House Marcerin. Dots pulsed across system maps, red and gold and gray, like sparks waiting for oxygen.

I sat across from Cersei. She looked even more withdrawn than usual—calm, but in that way, she gets when she's thinking ten moves ahead and losing sleep over only five of them.

"The scans confirm it," she said, pointing at the Selari corridor. "Marcerin's adaptive fleets are calibrating against our geothermal shadow patterns. They're testing how fast our armor can compensate."

Minister Kaelen frowned. "They shouldn't even be able to map that. Our tech is lineage-locked. Their AI—"

"Is learning," Cersei said.

I looked at the display. Red dots blinked near the fault lines beneath the eastern defense ranges.

"We trained for this," said Commander Ysra from across the room. "Valerius tech was built for endurance. Heat-siphon plating. Cryo-adaptive lining. No one outlasts us in this terrain."

"No one ever fought us with Marcerin's precision," Cersei replied.

There it was again—that edge in her voice. Not panic. Not fear. Just calculation under pressure.

"Marcerin's inheritance system is synthetic," she continued. "Most of their elite soldiers aren't born—they're programmed. Genetic enhancement. Bio-reinforcement. Field-ready by age twelve."

She tapped the display. "Their ships don't need pilots. Their scouts don't sleep. And their new combat AIs are learning how to mimic heat dispersion."

Silence held.

"Then we stop adapting," I said. "We strike."

The words were out before I'd meant them to be. Everyone turned.

Cersei looked at me, unreadable. Then—almost imperceptibly—she nodded.

"Finally," she said.

Afterward, Lyra walked with me through the northern corridor. The walls here were older—lined with frost-choked carvings and emblems so worn you had to know what they once were to see them clearly now.

"You spoke up," she said.

"I was tired of listening."

She gave me a sideways glance. "Or you finally heard yourself."

I didn't reply. My thoughts were drifting again—fracturing at the edges. The voice hadn't returned in full, but I felt its presence now, like pressure behind my eyes. Cold. Curious. Waiting.

We passed a glass vault sealed behind frost-rimmed locks. Inside, an old Valerius glacial spear hung suspended—its handle etched with pulse-wire and bio signs.

"Only works for your bloodline," Lyra said. "Same with half the weapons in the relic vault. They bind to heartbeat resonance."

"Legacy tech," I murmured. "Things we don't even understand anymore."

"You understand enough," she said. "They respond to you. They always have."

I looked at the spear.

It didn't feel like inheritance.

It felt like expectation.

The training yard was quiet that evening. Just me and Ysra.

She didn't speak much. Just handed me two short blades and gestured toward the stone ring. This time, there were no training guards watching. Just the two of us beneath the frozen stars.

We circled each other in silence.

Then she attacked.

I dodged.

Blocked.

Moved.

And then... something slipped.

Not my footing.

Time.

Her strike slowed in front of me—just for a moment. Just long enough to see the wind trail behind the arc of her blade. Long enough to step sideways before the blow landed.

I blinked.

She was already behind me, and I hadn't seen her move.

"Again," she said, frowning.

It happened twice more.

Until she stopped.

"You felt it," she said.

I said nothing.

"I don't know what that was," she continued. "And I've been fighting since before your sister could walk."

She turned away. "Whatever it is—you need to learn what side of you it comes from."

That night, I couldn't sleep.

Again.

I stood at the mirror.

And for the first time, I noticed the difference.

My reflection didn't move in sync. Just by a fraction of a second. Barely there. But enough.

Enough to know I wasn't imagining it.

Enough to know something inside me was trying to catch up—or get ahead.

Then the voice came back.

Low.

Measured.

"You are unraveling. That is good."

I swallowed.

"You have only just remembered what you are."

I didn't ask who it was.

Because deep down, I already knew—

It was not a stranger.

Chapter 10: The Crown Without Flame

The walls of the king's private war chamber were older than the rest of the palace—older even than the throne itself. They bore the marks of generations: cracked stone, faded banners, steel plates scorched by long-extinct weapons. No light came from the ceiling. Only the slow-burning embers of the hearth, and the faint blue glow of the map table in the center of the room.

Cersei stood just inside the doorway, her hands behind her back.

King Thalos did not look up.

He stood with one hand on the table, staring down at the projections—shifting battle maps, terrain scans, the red arc of Marcerin's push across the corridor.

"They've accelerated," she said.

"I know."

"They'll move to encircle the frost line. Take the high ranges first. Cut us off from the outer pass."

Thalos's jaw tensed. "Let them. Let them overreach."

Cersei stepped closer. "The council expects us to respond."

"The council expects nothing," Thalos said. "They exist to react. I exist to decide."

She didn't answer.

He looked up finally, eyes pale and sharp in the firelight.

"You disagreed with the boy."

Cersei's voice didn't waver. "He's not ready to command."

"He doesn't need to be ready. He needs to be feared."

She met his gaze. "Fear won't hold this house together."

"Honor won't hold it at all."

Silence again.

Thalos walked slowly to the far wall. He passed beneath a shattered sword mounted in dark iron. The blade had belonged to his father. Or so the stories said.

"I built this house from the bones of better men," he said. "Stronger men. I buried my father beneath the cold because he hesitated when he should have struck."

"You think I'll hesitate?" Cersei asked.

"I think you'll question," Thalos replied. "And questions are the beginning of cracks."

Cersei looked down at the map table. The red spread of Marcerin's forces had widened since she arrived.

"He's changing," she said. "Noctis. He's—different."

Thalos nodded once. "The frost remembers who it belongs to. Sooner or later, the blood wakes up."

Cersei hesitated. Then, "Do you believe in the prophecy?"

"No."

"Then what do you believe in?"

He turned back toward her.

"In what I can hold. What I can shape. And what I can destroy, if needed."

He stepped into the light again, towering without armor.

"If your brother fails," Thalos said, "I'll break him. Quietly. Before the world sees."

Cersei didn't flinch. "And if he doesn't fail?"

Thalos paused.

Then, softly: "Then I'll begin to wonder who he's becoming."

The chamber aboard the Sable Veil was lined with black-tinted glass, its windows displaying the vast emptiness of space punctuated by the soft glow of stars. Below, the snowy sprawl of Erythra hung like a bruise beneath frost—silent, ancient, watching.

Lucien Marcerin stood with his hands clasped behind his back, posture elegant and composed, even in solitude.

The silence here was different. Not the kind bred from tension or reverence like in Valerius halls, but one cultivated—measured. Like everything else in his house.

A soft chime sounded.

He didn't turn.

"Enter."

The door hissed open. A figure in Marcerin-gray stepped inside: angular armor, clean-lined, not a scratch out of place. His steward, Commander Solen.

"They've rejected the offer," Solen said, voice flat.

Lucien didn't react. He had expected as much.

"And the movement?"

"Valerius has begun repositioning defense fleets. Standard thermal shielding patterns. Crude but effective in polar range."

Lucien nodded once. "Let them entrench. Their strength has always been their stillness."

He tapped a control at his wrist. A tactical projection bloomed in the air before him—valleys, fault lines, known outposts. Lines of red marked the Selari corridor, looping like veins ready to be severed.

"Let's test how deep their patience runs."

Solen hesitated. "And your father?"

Lucien's jaw tensed. He walked slowly toward the glass, watching the white gleam of Erythra shift under orbital rotation.

"He wants spectacle," Lucien said. "He believes fear brings compliance."

"And you don't?"

Lucien turned now. His eyes were sharp, almost luminous beneath the room's pale lighting.

"I believe in precision."

He paused.

"Fear burns quickly. Precision corrodes."

Hours later, Lucien sat alone in his private quarters, the armor removed, replaced with a high-collared gray coat. In front of him, a simple datapad glowed with an open file.

A still image.

Cersei Valerius, standing in the council hall. Head high. Unbent.

Lucien stared at the image; expression unreadable.

Then he swiped it away.

Another image loaded.

Noctis.

Younger. From a royal ceremony years ago—standing beside him, laughing about something now long forgotten.

Lucien exhaled slowly.

"You were never supposed to matter," he murmured.

The shadows in the room flickered slightly as the ship adjusted orbital drift.

Lucien stood.

He walked to a smaller display and opened a private file—unmarked, untraceable.

Inside: telemetry, gene pattern records, and fractured bits of encoded prophecy texts.

At the top, a phrase written in ancient script:

The Coldborn Flame shall rise from the house of winter, but the ash shall answer to another.

Lucien closed the file.

His reflection stared back at him in the blackened glass.

Still.

Perfect.

And patient.

I found Elias in the old chapel.

It was carved into the side of the mountain, hidden beneath the palace's eastern wing—built from black stone and glass like everything else in Erythra, but quieter, older. Dust caught the light like snow that had forgotten how to fall.

He was seated on one of the low benches, his robes draped around him like layers of shadow. He didn't look up when I entered.

"You're late," he said softly.

"I wasn't told to come."

"You weren't. But you came anyway."

I sat across from him. The silence stretched. Outside, wind howled through the narrow gaps in the rock.

"Do you believe it?" I asked.

Elias didn't answer right away.

"The prophecy?" I clarified. "Ith'Kaladrin. The Coldborn Flame. All of it."

Elias finally turned to look at me. His eyes were calm—not like water, but like the stillness that comes after a storm has already passed.

"I believe in patterns," he said. "I believe in echoes. And I believe that sometimes… the world remembers itself through people."

"That's not an answer."

"No," he agreed. "It's a warning."

I leaned forward, elbows on my knees.

"They're saying it more often," I said. "The servants. The officers. Even some of the council. They think I'm him."

"And do you?"

I didn't respond.

Elias watched me closely. "You've felt it, haven't you? The shift. The weight. The sense that something in you isn't quite yours anymore."

I swallowed. "It's a voice."

He didn't look surprised. Only thoughtful.

"It will offer you many things," he said. "Some true. Most not. But all of them dangerous."

"What is it?"

He looked away, toward the empty altar at the front of the chapel. A simple slab of stone. No symbols. No names.

"Once," he said, "the Witness was said to be a memory—of the first storm, the first silence, the first sorrow. Not a god. Not a demon. Just… the echo of what we lost when we learned to be more than we were."

"That's not possible," I said.

"It's not meant to be."

He turned back to me.

"You don't have to become anything, Noctis. But you will be asked. Again, and again."

"And if I say no?"

Elias smiled faintly. "Then you remain yourself."

"And if I say yes?"

The smile faded.

"Then the world will follow you. Or burn trying to catch up."

Chapter 11: A Blade Without a Name

The transport skiff hummed low beneath our boots as we broke through the upper clouds of Erythra's eastern ridge. White and gray peeled away, revealing the jagged terrain below—spires of black ice, rivers frozen mid-flow, and the distant outline of the relay tower we were sent to investigate.

My first sanctioned deployment.

No one said it out loud. But I saw it in the way the guards looked at me. Heard it in the quiet tension of the command officer's voice when she briefed the team. Not quite reverence. Not quite suspicion. Something colder. Like I was a weapon they hadn't decided to unsheathe.

Lyra stood beside me.

She was in full field gear now—sleek frost plate armor, matte-black with minimal markings. Her hair was braided tight against her scalp, and her expression was unreadable as always. But I noticed the way her hand rested just slightly closer to her blade than usual.

"Something feels off," I murmured.

"We haven't landed yet."

"That's not what I meant."

She glanced at me, just once. "Then you're learning."

The relay station was dead.

No heat signatures. No active pings. The signal drop had been flagged by orbital patrol twelve hours prior. We were the response.

The guards fanned out quickly. I moved slower, eyes tracking the ruins.

The building had been sheared clean through, like something had cut it with surgical precision. Not an explosion—no scorched edges. No scatter. Just silence.

Lyra crouched beside one of the split walls.

"Too clean," she said.

I nodded.

We stepped deeper inside. Frost clung to the interior surfaces like it had been dragged inward unnaturally—reaching across wiring and broken consoles like veins.

Then I felt it.

A tug.

Like a thread behind my eyes being pulled taut.

The room wavered. Not visually. Not physically. Just... temporally. Like the present was hesitating.

Lyra straightened suddenly. Her eyes widened—not with fear, but confusion.

"Did you hear that?"

I hadn't heard anything.

But I knew exactly what she meant.

We stepped further in—and the moment we crossed the next threshold, everything stopped.

Just for a second.

A breath.

A flicker.

Then the world snapped back. The wind returned. The snow shifted. The flickering light from above stuttered twice and held steady.

Lyra turned to me. "What was that?"

I opened my mouth to speak—and felt something crawl beneath my skin.

A whisper, almost too soft to catch:

"You are reaching."

I flinched.

Lyra's hand was on her blade in a blink.

"What did you hear?" she asked.

I shook my head. "Nothing."

She didn't believe me.

But she didn't press.

We returned hours later, silent most of the flight.

The report went up the chain quickly—unexplained damage, temporal instability, no survivors. No clear enemy trace. Cersei would read between the lines.

Back in the palace, I stepped into the chapel again.

Elias was already waiting.

He didn't ask questions.

Didn't offer comfort.

He simply said, "It's begun, then."

I sat on the bench across from him. "What did I see out there?"

"Possibility," he said. "Friction. You're pulling at the seam between time and choice."

"It didn't feel like a choice."

"It rarely does."

I looked down at my hands. They were steady. But inside, I felt like a mirror someone had just breathed on—fogged, trembling, unfinished.

Elias stood.

He walked to the altar, touched one hand to the cold stone, then turned back to me.

"You're not a prince anymore," he said.

"Then what am I?"

He met my gaze.

"A blade," he said.

And left before I could ask... whose.

Chapter 11: A Blade Without a Name

The transport skiff hummed low beneath our boots as we broke through the upper clouds of Erythra's eastern ridge. White and gray peeled away, revealing the jagged terrain below—spires of black ice, rivers frozen mid-flow, and the distant outline of the relay tower we were sent to investigate.

My first sanctioned deployment.

No one said it out loud. But I saw it in the way the guards looked at me. Heard it in the quiet tension of the command officer's voice when she briefed the team. Not quite reverence. Not quite suspicion. Something colder. Like I was a weapon they hadn't decided to unsheathe.

Lyra stood beside me.

She was in full field gear now—sleek frost plate armor, matte-black with minimal markings. Her hair was braided tight against her scalp, and her expression was unreadable as always. But I noticed the way her hand rested just slightly closer to her blade than usual.

"Something feels off," I murmured.

"We haven't landed yet."

"That's not what I meant."

She glanced at me, just once. "Then you're learning."

The relay station was dead.

No heat signatures. No active pings. The signal drop had been flagged by orbital patrol twelve hours prior. We were the response.

The guards fanned out quickly. I moved slower, eyes tracking the ruins.

The building had been sheared clean through, like something had cut it with surgical precision. Not an explosion—no scorched edges. No scatter. Just silence.

Lyra crouched beside one of the split walls.

"Too clean," she said.

I nodded.

We stepped deeper inside. Frost clung to the interior surfaces like it had been dragged inward unnaturally reaching across wiring and broken consoles like veins.

Then I felt it.

A tug.

Like a thread behind my eyes being pulled taut.

The room wavered. Not visually. Not physically. Just... temporally. Like the present was hesitating.

Lyra straightened suddenly. Her eyes widened—not with fear, but confusion.

"Did you hear that?"

I hadn't heard anything.

But I knew exactly what she meant.

We stepped further in—and the moment we crossed the next threshold, everything stopped.

Just for a second.

A breath.

A flicker.

Then the world snapped back. The wind returned. The snow shifted. The flickering light from above stuttered twice and held steady.

Lyra turned to me. "What was that?"

I opened my mouth to speak—and felt something crawl beneath my skin.

A whisper, almost too soft to catch:

"You are reaching."

I flinched.

Lyra's hand was on her blade in a blink.

"What did you hear?" she asked.

I shook my head. "Nothing."

She didn't believe me.

But she didn't press.

We returned hours later, silent most of the flight.

The report went up the chain quickly unexplained damage, temporal instability, no survivors. No clear enemy trace. Cersei would read between the lines.

Back in the palace, I stepped into the chapel again.

Elias was already waiting.

He didn't ask questions.

Didn't offer comfort.

He simply said, "It's begun, then."

I sat on the bench across from him. "What did I see out there?"

"Possibility," he said. "Friction. You're pulling at the seam between time and choice."

"It didn't feel like a choice."

"It rarely does."

I looked down at my hands. They were steady. But inside, I felt like a mirror someone had just breathed on—fogged, trembling, unfinished.

Elias stood.

He walked to the altar, touched one hand to the cold stone, then turned back to me.

"You're not a prince anymore," he said.

"Then what am I?"

He met my gaze.

"A blade," he said.

And left before I could ask... whose.

(Cersei)

The report lay open on the war table, its contents scrolling in slow, pulsing light.

Cersei stood motionless beside it. One hand on the edge of the table. The other clenched behind her back.

No survivors.

No heat signatures.

Temporal instability reported but not confirmed.

She read it again.

And again.

It wasn't the dead station that disturbed her. It wasn't the silence. It was the language.

The pauses in the logs.

The inconsistencies in how time had been recorded by the skiff's instruments.

It was subtle. But it was there.

Like something behind the report was watching her read it.

She turned away from the table and looked out the tall slit of the frost-glass window. Snow drifted beyond the walls. The mountains remained still.

But something else was moving now.

And it had her brother's shadow.

(Lyra)

"I don't know what it was."

Ysra didn't respond. Just kept sharpening the edge of her blade with slow, practiced movements.

Lyra stood with her arms folded, still in her field uniform. She hadn't slept since they returned. She wasn't sure she could.

"He heard something," she said. "I don't know what. But something changed in the room. For a second... it felt like the air forgot how to move."

Ysra looked up.

"You think it was him?"

"I think it wasn't just him."

That got a nod.

Ysra set the blade aside. "You're his shadow, Cael. Until he breaks, or bends. Or becomes something else."

Lyra's voice was quiet.

"What if he already has?"

(Lucien)

The data came encrypted. Narrow beam signal. Private relay. Eyes-only.

Lucien stood in the command alcove of the Sable Veil, hands behind his back, as the message unfolded before him.

Relay destroyed.

No traceable weapon signature.

Marcerin scout teams had logged an anomalous energy pulse just beyond the border. Brief. Controlled. Unnatural.

Lucien smiled.

Not wide.

Not warm.

Just enough.

"It's beginning," he said to the empty room.

He closed the message. Turned to a locked drawer beneath the projection table. Entered a six-digit code.

The drawer opened with a hiss.

Inside: a black case, smaller than a palm. Cold to the touch.

He stared at it for a long moment.

Then closed the drawer.

Not yet.

Chapter 12: The Widening Vein

The descent into the ancestral sanctum was silent.

Stone steps carved into the bedrock curved downward, lit only by faint silver braziers burning cold fire. The walls narrowed with every turn, until even the echoes of our boots seemed to fade. It was not the cold that unnerved me—but the weight. Like the air itself remembered too much.

Cersei walked ahead of me. She hadn't said a word since summoning me from training that morning.

We stopped at a sealed archway, half-buried in frost.

Cersei pressed her palm against the plate beside it.

It read her instantly.

The door opened with a low groan.

Inside, the room pulsed.

The chamber was circular, ringed with relics—weapon hilts, frozen armor, shattered helms—all mounted in silent display. But these weren't for decoration. These were legacies. Each artifact tied to a Valerius heir who had once walked the path I now stood on.

At the center of the chamber stood a raised platform. Embedded into it: a dormant blade. Long, elegant, forged from a dark alloy that shimmered with hints of frost light. Not ceremonial.

Functional.

Cersei gestured. "Step forward."

I did.

"Place your hand on the pommel."

I hesitated.

"This is tradition," she said. "Every heir is tested by it. It bonds to your blood. Nothing more."

I stepped forward. Raised my hand.

Then—

The moment I touched the blade, the air bent.

The chamber pulsed. Not light. Not sound. Just... presence.

The braziers flickered out.

Frost leapt from the walls to the floor.

And the blade, dormant for centuries, began to hum.

Not in sound.

In memory.

Images surged behind my eyes—too fast to grasp. Snowstorms. Battles. A woman crying in silence. My own hands, covered in blood I hadn't spilled yet.

And then—

A voice.

"She doubts you."

I turned my head sharply.

Cersei hadn't moved. But her hand had drifted toward her waist—toward the dagger she always wore beneath her coat.

"She fears what you will become. All they do."

"Would you protect her?"

I felt the energy swell in my chest. Not heat. Not power. Something colder. Sharper.

The blade beneath my hand sang—and every relic on the walls trembled.

Cersei stepped forward.

"Noctis," she said. Firm. Focused. "Let go."

"Or will you choose freedom?"

"And bury her like the rest?"

The pressure built.

I gritted my teeth. My hand ached.

And then—

I released it.

The chamber fell still.

The braziers flared back to life.

Frost retreated.

The blade dimmed.

Cersei said nothing for a long time.

Then: "It responded."

I nodded.

She turned away. But not before I caught it—the briefest flicker of something in her eyes.

Not fear.

Not pride.

Something in between.

And then she said, quietly, "You'll need to leave the palace. Soon."

"Why?"

"Because whatever this is…" She looked back at the blade. "It doesn't belong here anymore."

Neither do you, I heard her think.

But she didn't say it.

She didn't have to.

Chapter 14: The Fire Behind Silence

We were told it was a forward strike team.

Marcerin soldiers breaching Valerius space through the old snowfields—testing our reach, provoking a response. I was sent with a squad of twelve. Lyra came without being ordered. I didn't ask why. I knew.

The location was a mining settlement long abandoned—at least, that's what we believed. The signal disruption had been brief, faint. But something in it caught

Cersei's attention. And now I was here, breathing frost and tension while the wind whispered around broken structures half-buried in ice.

"They're not here," said one of the guards after a sweep.

"They were," Lyra replied, crouching near a heat signature buried beneath a collapsed roof. "Hours ago. Maybe less."

I stared into the dark between buildings. The place felt... haunted. Not by ghosts. By decisions waiting to be made.

We moved deeper.

And that's when we found them.

Not soldiers.

Refugees.

A dozen at least. Huddled in a broken shelter, shivering in silence. Most of them unarmed. Half-starved. Wearing Marcerin livery, yes—but not military. Workers. Maybe engineers. Maybe scientists. One child.

They looked up at us with wide eyes and frostbitten skin.

Lyra stepped forward first. "We were told this was a strike team," she said, low.

The oldest of them—a man with trembling hands and a stitched wound above his eye—spoke carefully.

"We defected," he said. "Left the research station when the weapons tests began. We didn't want—"

A sudden pulse behind my eyes.

The voice.

"They will report you. They will betray you. They will run back to the fire that forged them."

"End it. You know what must be done."

I staggered.

Lyra turned. "Noctis—?"

The ground felt wrong. The cold deeper. The air still.

"Protect your sister. Your people. Your name. Do not hesitate."

My heart pounded.

I saw the flash of future—just a glimpse. The older man speaking to a Marcerin officer. Describing me. My power. My hesitation.

Then another vision—Valerius ships burning. Frost turned to flame.

I looked down at my hands.

They were glowing.

Not with heat.

With memory.

"You have one choice. Do not fail it."

"Noctis." Lyra's voice now. Sharper. Closer.

"They're not threats," she said. "They're people."

She stepped between me and the refugees.

And I saw it.

Another flicker. Another thread of possibility.

Lyra dead.

Cersei bleeding.

Marcerin fleets closing in.

I took a breath.

And I let it go.

The frost exploded outward.

Silent.

Precise.

By the time it faded, the shelter was buried in stillness. The air tasted of iron and snow.

I stood in the center of it.

Alone.

Even with Lyra still watching.

She didn't speak.

Not at first.

Then: "You didn't have to."

I didn't answer.

There was nothing I could say.

Back at the palace, I gave my report.

"Intruders neutralized."

No one asked questions.

Not then.

But I saw the look in Cersei's eyes when she read the full logs.

And I saw the way Lyra wouldn't meet mine.

That night, I stood before the mirror again.

The frost didn't creep this time.

It formed.

Clean lines. Circles. Symbols.

"You chose well," the voice said.

And I felt something in me go quiet.

Not because it was over.

Because it had just begun.

Chapter 15: Cold Ashes

The palace halls felt different now.

Colder, somehow. Not in temperature—but in weight. Every glance I caught from the guards, the servants, even the officers who used to nod when I passed... was shorter. Sharper. Less certain.

The silence followed me through every corridor.

And Lyra didn't.

Not since the mission.

She still reported for duty. Still stood when summoned. Still followed orders. But the quiet between us had changed. It wasn't tense—it was hollow. Like something had cracked beneath the surface and neither of us wanted to see how deep it went.

Cersei summoned me the morning after.

The war chamber was empty but for her, one hand on the table, the other holding the datapad containing my report.

She didn't offer a greeting.

"You lied," she said.

I didn't respond.

Her voice was calm. I almost wished it wasn't.

"They weren't soldiers. The logs confirm it. Civilian bio-signatures. Unarmed. You knew."

"I made a choice."

"You made a mistake."

I met her eyes. "They would've run. Told Marcerin what they saw. What I am. You've seen the simulations."

"I've also seen what restraint looks like," she said. "You're not the only Valerius who's faced impossible odds."

"But I'm the only one with this."

I didn't mean to raise my voice.

But the chamber caught it—threw it back at me from every wall.

Cersei didn't flinch.

"Noctis," she said. "I want you to listen very carefully."

She stepped closer.

"You are still my brother. You are still part of this house. But if you begin making decisions that risk turning this family into a symbol of terror instead of strength... I will stop you. Do you understand?"

I did.

And yet—

"She will abandon you when it matters."

The voice again.

Faint.

Not cruel. Just... inevitable.

I stepped back.

"I need air."

Cersei didn't stop me.

She just turned back to the table and said, without looking, "So do we all."

I found Lyra outside the west barracks.

She was running drills with the other guards, blade in hand, focused, relentless.

I waited until they cleared.

She didn't acknowledge me. Not until I spoke.

"I thought you believed in me."

She didn't turn. "I did."

"Then why won't you look at me?"

"Because I don't know who I'm looking at anymore."

The words struck deeper than I expected.

I stepped closer. "I did what I had to."

"No," she said. "You did what you wanted. You let it speak for you."

There was a pause. Her shoulders tightened.

"Was I wrong?" I asked. "About them? About what would've happened?"

"Maybe not," she said quietly. "But you made the decision like it didn't matter either way."

She turned to face me.

Her eyes were tired.

"You asked why I stayed," she said. "It wasn't loyalty. It was hope."

She walked past me without another word.

And this time—I didn't follow.

That night, the frost didn't whisper.

It pressed.

It pushed.

The symbols on the mirror were gone.

Only a single word remained, etched in ice:

Soon.

I stared at it for a long time.

Then I let the frost take the room.

And closed my eyes.

Chapter 16: The Knife That Waits

The chamber aboard the Sable Veil was dark but alive with light.

Holograms flickered in slow orbit around Lucien—maps, telemetry, heat signatures, and filtered reports sent from a dozen fronts. But his eyes weren't on the data.

They were on the still image in the center of the room.

Noctis.

Captured from a distant surveillance drone—standing amid a frozen field, eyes unreadable, surrounded by corpses rimmed in ice.

A single command had turned refugees into ruin.

Lucien studied the image for a long moment.

"He's accelerating," *he murmured.*

Commander Solen stepped into the chamber. She said nothing, waiting just beyond the edge of the light.

"He wasn't supposed to be a soldier," *Lucien continued.* "He was a rumor. A warning. A shadow in the high snow. But now…"

He turned to Solen.

"Now he's becoming something else."

"We can move against him," *she said.* "If we strike—"

"No."

Lucien waved the suggestion away.

"Not yet."

He walked to the edge of the display and tapped a command.

New projections blinked into place—Noctis's confirmed deployments, his known power spikes, predictive behavior mapping.

"Have the analysts update the probability grid," *Lucien said.* "Factor in religious adoption curves. The Solariate is spreading faster than we expected."

"Yes, my lord."

"And initiate Protocol Hollow. Quietly. One agent."

Solen hesitated.

"That's a ghost order," she said. "It hasn't been used in—"

"I know," Lucien said. "We'll send them to observe. Not engage. If Noctis crosses a second line, I want to be ready before he becomes a god."

He turned back to the image.

"And if he already has?"

Solen's voice was quiet. "Then we'll need a different kind of knife."

Lucien didn't answer.

He just watched the frozen stillness of the field.

And whispered:

"Let's see what he becomes."

Chapter 17: Trial of Silence

The hidden archive beneath the palace had no name.

It was older than the war. Older than the Valerius line, if the stonework could be trusted. Built into the roots of Erythra's foundation, where warmth never touched and silence pressed inward like a second skin.

Elias descended alone.

No guards.

No torchlight.

Only the flickering silver glow of the ancient glyphs etched into the stairwell walls—Solariate script, written in a language no longer taught aloud. A tongue preserved only for scripture, prophecy, and warnings too dangerous to remember.

He carried a single sealed scroll. And a key only he possessed.

At the final threshold, the wall recognized his presence and split open with a hiss of frost and dust. The chamber beyond lit slowly—arcane light pooling in the air like memory.

Elias stepped inside.

Shelves curved upward like ribs, filled with crystal plates, carved tablets, and whisper-slates long disconnected from surface networks. This was where the old prophecies slept. The ones the Solariate did not chant in public halls. The ones kept behind silence.

He approached the central podium and unrolled the scroll.

It was a copy. The original had burned with a temple long lost to time. But the words remained etched into his memory.

"The Coldborn Flame shall walk among frost, not fire. But the silent hour shall break him from within."

"And if the blade that sleeps awakens too soon, the crown shall fall not to blood... but to silence."

He exhaled.

The meaning wasn't clear.

But something was wrong. Something was always missing.

He turned to the wall of mirrored plates.

Each one a reflection of part of the Solariate vision. Shattered glimpses. Incomplete verses.

And then—he found it.

A fragment he hadn't read since his ordination.

It was faint, nearly unreadable beneath centuries of damage. But the glyphs were clear enough.

"He who bears the witness shall not be the heir."

"But the echo of a buried god."

Elias stepped back.

"Noctis…"

He closed his eyes.

The Solariate had been pushing his name into the winds for years now. Whispering it into sermons, embedding it into hymns. Not at his command—but with his silence.

And in that silence, something darker had taken root.

He left the scroll. Sealed the room.

And when he returned to the chapel above, he did not kneel.

He only whispered:

"If I have helped create a god…, may I have the courage to stop him."

Chapter 18: The Ice March

Scene One: Spectators of the Storm

The training hall was sealed.

Stone walls swallowed every sound like snowbanks, muting even the clash of boots or the hum of energy that buzzed just beneath the floor. Wards pulsed faintly along the arches—old protection glyphs meant to keep the worst accidents from becoming headlines.

I stood alone in the center circle.

Three elite guards ringed me—silent, waiting, tense.

Above, on the balcony, Cersei watched. She didn't speak. She didn't need to. She was the one who called for this. "Evaluation," she said. Not a challenge. Not a test. Just… clarity.

And beside her stood our father.

King Thalos.

His arms were crossed. His face carved from the same stone as the walls.

He hadn't come to watch me train since I was twelve.

Ysra stood at the edge of the circle. "Begin when ready."

I didn't wait.

I stepped forward.

The first guard moved fast—sharp, trained, clean. But I didn't need speed. Just timing.

As we crossed, I let the world slow. Just a hair. A ripple. His strike lagged by a fraction.

I slid under it and brought my blade up into his ribs—flat side. Hard. He dropped.

The other two came at once.

I didn't flinch.

I stepped through their rhythm—folded time like a cloak and slipped past the moment they'd chosen. Their blades bit empty air. I moved through the gap, pivoted, and knocked both down in silence.

Ten seconds.

That's all it took.

I looked up to the balcony.

Cersei didn't blink.

Ysra nodded. "Again."

The guards rose.

But this time—she joined them.

"You too?" I asked.

"I want to feel it for myself."

I gave her a nod.

And then she came at me like winter.

Fast. Precise. No hesitation. No telegraph.

She didn't fight like a bodyguard. She fought like someone who had carved herself into a weapon long before she'd ever been assigned to protect one.

I backed up quickly—her strikes were aimed at pressure points, weak joints, balance lines.

She knew where to break me.

And still—

I stopped time.

Just for a breath.

Enough to move where she couldn't follow.

When it resumed, her sword swept through empty air.

Mine was already at her shoulder.

She stilled.

Lowered her weapon.

Match over.

Above us, my father finally spoke.

"He doesn't fight like a prince."

"No," Cersei said. "He fights like something trying not to become a god."

Scene Two: Steel and Thread

I walked the west corridor alone after the match.

Footsteps joined me halfway down. I didn't turn.

Cersei.

She matched my pace. We said nothing for a time.

"You didn't look human down there," she finally said.

"I'm not sure I am anymore."

She didn't argue.

We passed beneath a high arch of snow lit glass. The light was dull but clear—the kind you only get after a storm has passed and left everything still.

"What did he think?" I asked.

"Father?" she said. "He's trying to decide if you're an asset... or a threat."

"And you?"

"I'm trying to decide which answer I want."

I let out a breath. "If you ever decide I'm a threat, what happens?"

"I'll try to stop you," she said. "Without killing you, if I can."

I nodded. "That's fair."

We kept walking.

But we didn't look at each other again.

Scene Three: The March

The call came twelve hours later.

A breach at the Selen Pass. Marcerin scouts moving too close—likely probing the infrastructure relay. If they froze it, half our eastward communications would collapse.

I was deployed with two airskiffs and fifty elites.

The storm started an hour in. Dense. Unnatural. I knew the moment it hit that it wasn't random.

The first bodies dropped when one of our own turned traitor.

Three guards. Dead before we even reached the ridge.

I stopped holding back.

The storm couldn't touch me.

I moved through it—folded it around me like second skin. I felt the weight of every heartbeat, every breath, every possible failure.

The enemy was waiting near the ridge.

They never saw me coming.

But it wasn't them that nearly broke us.

It was the trap.

The ice had been fractured beneath our path—engineered to split and swallow. I watched four Valerius soldiers fall before I realized what was happening.

I heard screaming.

Then the voice.

"Would you see it undone?"

"Yes," I said.

"Then let it end."

I moved.

Time bent.

Snowflakes hung motionless midair.

I walked to the breach—through frozen screams and suspended panic. I raised my hand.

The ice responded.

It surged. Not wild. Not chaotic. Exact. It sealed the breach. Closed the cracks. Swallowed the bodies.

I don't know if they were still alive.

I didn't ask.

We flew back in silence.

No one looked at me.

No one spoke.

When I stood beneath the high mirrors of the great hall again, I waited.

For Cersei. For my father. For judgment.

None came.

Only the snow.

And the voice.

"There is no path back. Only through."

Chapter 19: In Her Shadow

I used to think the snow was colder the year my mother died.

Memory twists things. Makes them heavier. Sharper around the edges. But some things stayed clear, no matter how many storms passed.

I remember the day she was buried beneath the frostline of Erythra's northern ridge.

The sky was clear.

The kind of clear that makes you feel small. Like even the planet had nothing left to say.

Cersei stood beside me.

I was barely more than a boy—thirteen, maybe. Still too young to understand what a throne demanded. Too soft to realize what it cost.

But she knew.

She didn't cry at the funeral. She didn't flinch when they lowered our mother into the frozen crypts. She only watched. Still. Silent. A blade she hadn't drawn yet.

Afterward, the nobles spoke in careful circles around us. Whispering about succession. About futures. About how House Valerius would endure.

I hid behind Cersei's shadow, listening.

Afraid.

It wasn't until later, when the halls had emptied and the frost candles guttered low, that she found me.

I was sitting on the edge of the empty throne dais, legs swinging uselessly, eyes burning from holding back tears.

Cersei sat beside me.

For a long time, neither of us said anything.

Then she pulled a chain from her neck—a simple band of silver, rough with wear. She pressed it into my hand.

"Our mother wore this when she was crowned," she said. "She gave it to me the night before she died."

I tried to give it back.

She closed my fingers over it.

"Noctis," she said, her voice quiet but unshakable. "You don't have to be ready yet. You don't have to be strong yet."

She looked out at the vast emptiness of the great hall.

"But one day, you will be. And when that day comes, you'll need to remember something."

I waited.

She met my eyes—hers clear, cold, burning.

"You're not the crown. You're the fire beneath it. And when they try to freeze you into what they want you to be... burn colder."

I didn't understand what she meant then.

Not really.

But I nodded.

And I kept the chain.

Now, years later, standing alone beneath those same hollow arches, I understood too well.

Cersei hadn't protected me out of duty.

She had protected the idea of me—the boy our mother had believed in.

But that boy was long buried beneath the ice.

And all that remained was what the snow hadn't managed to kill.

Me.

Chapter 20: The Flicker and the Flame

The days after the Ice March passed like smoke.

No one said my name when I entered a room. Not the guards. Not the council scribes. Not even the acolytes of the Solariate who once bowed low when I passed.

I wasn't exiled.

I wasn't punished.

But I could feel it—the quiet. Heavy as armor. Thicker than the cold.

Victory had a taste like blood.

And the halls of Valerius tasted of it now.

I found Lyra by the eastern gate.

She wasn't supposed to be there—her shift had ended hours ago. But she stood with her back to the stone, arms folded, looking out over the endless plains where the snow swallowed the horizon.

I approached slowly.

She didn't turn.

"You should be inside," I said.

"Should be," she answered.

We stood there for a long time, not speaking. Watching the wind scrape lines into the drifts.

Finally, I said, "You blame me."

"I don't have the right to blame you."

"You think what I did was wrong."

She didn't answer immediately.

Then: "I think you stopped asking yourself if it mattered."

The words stung, sharper than any blade.

I stepped closer. Close enough that the breath between us clouded the air.

"I made the only choice I could," I said.

"You made the choice that was easiest," she whispered. "Easiest for who you're becoming. Not for the boy I knew."

I didn't know what to say to that.

She turned to me at last—really turned. Her eyes weren't angry. They were hollow.

"I stayed," she said. "Longer than I should have. Hoping there was still enough of him left."

"Lyra—"

She shook her head.

"I'm not leaving my post. Not yet. But whatever you're turning into… it's not something I can follow."

I looked at her, trying to find the words that could unmake what I had done.

There weren't any.

The wind howled through the gates.

"You should go inside," she said again, softer this time.

I didn't move.

She didn't wait.

Lyra disappeared into the snow like a ghost, leaving only footprints that the storm would soon erase.

That night, the frost didn't creep against the windows.

It shattered them.

Hairline fractures across every mirror. Cracks threading through glass that once showed me who I was.

The Witness's voice drifted from the shards.

"They will not walk with you into the storm."

"So, you will walk alone."

I pressed my hand against the glass.

And for the first time, I didn't pull away.

Chapter 21: Echoes in the Blood

The snow fell heavier that night.

It blanketed the palace grounds in a silence so deep, even the thermal vents buried beneath the flagstones could do nothing to lift the chill.

I didn't sleep.

I couldn't.

The cracks in the mirror had deepened—thin lines spiderwebbing outward from where my hand had pressed against the glass the night Lyra left me standing in the storm.

I stared at the fractures, at the pieces of myself reflected a hundred ways.

And then the Witness spoke.

"You have seen only the surface."

The voice was closer than before.

Inside the room.

Inside me.

The frost on the mirror shifted—no longer random, but deliberate. A pattern emerged. A doorway carved from ice and shadow.

Without thinking, I stepped through it.

The world warped.

I stood in a place that smelled of blood and steel.

Not memory.

Memory rewritten.

A chamber lit by low, pulsing lights. Machines older than anything I had seen. Symbols I couldn't read, carved into the walls.

At the center of the room—an operating table.

A boy lay strapped to it.

Small. Frail.

His skin blistered from cold and something deeper, something that pulsed beneath it.

I took a step closer.

It was me.

I watched as figures in dark robes—faceless, voiceless—leaned over the boy. Injected something into his veins. Spoken words not meant for ears. Words that etched into bone and soul.

I tried to move forward, to tear them away—but I wasn't there. Only the Witness was.

"You were not born to power."

"You were carved into it."

The boy's eyes opened—wild, terrified.

They weren't my eyes.

Not yet.

But they would be.

The scene shifted.

Flashes.

A memory of Cersei, standing outside a sealed door, fists clenched, tears frozen to her cheeks.

A memory of King Thalos, watching through a glass wall as the experiments continued, his face unreadable.

A memory of the day they declared me "blessed."

The frost deepened.

The voice pressed closer.

"You were made for silence."

"You were made to end the line."

I fell backward out of the mirror-world, gasping.

The cracks in the glass bled frost onto the floor, threading out across the stone like veins.

I sank to my knees.

I didn't know how long I stayed there.

But when I rose, something inside me had gone quiet.

Not broken.

Just colder.

More certain.

Outside, the storm raged.

And in the heart of Erythra, the Silent Heir waited to be born.

Chapter 22: Ash on the Mountain

The banners of House Valerius snapped like wounded wings in the high wind.

I stood atop the eastern watchtower and watched them go.

King Thalos rode at the head of the procession—spear in hand, armor black against the gray of the storm. He didn't look back at the palace. He didn't need to. In his mind, the battle was already won. Victory was a matter of blood and stubbornness.

Cersei stood beside me; hands clenched around the railing until her knuckles blanched.

"He's making a mistake," she said.

I didn't argue.

She had already begged him not to go. Had cited the reports, the terrain, the timing.
Lucien's forces weren't trying to win the war outright. They were baiting us. They wanted him on the field.

He went anyway.

Because strength, to my father, was not just a tactic.

It was a religion.

The battle at the Sable Ridge should have been a slaughter.

On paper, we had the advantage—numbers, terrain, experience.

But paper burns.

I wasn't there when the lines collapsed.

I wasn't there when the Marcerin strike teams—silent, cloaked in frost armor—circled behind our forward units.

I only know what the survivors said later:

That the king fought like winter incarnate. That he shattered spears with his bare hands. That his roar cracked ice at the edges of the ridge.

And that when Lucien himself stepped onto the field, the air grew colder still.

It wasn't a duel.

It wasn't even a fair fight.

Lucien didn't fight for honor.

He fought to end a dynasty.

They say he didn't even draw a sword—just raised a hand, signaling his agents hidden among the Marcerin forces.

A pulse of sonic energy ruptured the ridge face.

The ice broke.

The mountain broke.

King Thalos fell with it.

They found him hours later.

Half-buried under crushed stone and twisted iron.

Still breathing.

Barely.

They brought him back under heavy guard.

Noctis Valerius—prince, soldier, inheritor—stood silent at the gates as the procession returned.

The healers said he was alive.

Said the machines were keeping his heart steady.

Said the old blood of Valerius still clung to life with teeth and broken nails.

But when I looked into his eyes—

I knew he was already gone.

Cersei took control the next morning.

No coronation.

No ceremony.

Just a command whispered down the halls:

"All decisions pass through Cersei Valerius now."

And the nobles obeyed.

Because when the heart of winter falls silent, you listen to the wind that remains.

I stood in the silent hall that night, staring at the empty throne.

And for the first time, I realized:

The throne wasn't empty.

It was waiting.

For me.

Or for the thing I was becoming.

The Witness stirred beneath my skin.

The frost crept higher on the mirrors.

And somewhere far beyond the frozen walls of Erythra, I imagined Lucien smiling.

Because he hadn't killed my father to take the throne.

He had killed him to leave it wide open.

And wide-open doors are invitations.

For gods.

Or monsters.

Or whatever I was becoming.

Chapter 22: Ash on the Mountain

The banners of House Valerius snapped like wounded wings in the high wind.

I stood atop the eastern watchtower and watched them go.

King Thalos rode at the head of the procession—spear in hand, armor black against the gray of the storm. He didn't look back at the palace. He didn't need to. In his mind, the battle was already won. Victory was a matter of blood and stubbornness.

Cersei stood beside me; hands clenched around the railing until her knuckles blanched.

"He's making a mistake," she said.

I didn't argue.

She had already begged him not to go. Had cited the reports, the terrain, the timing.
Lucien's forces weren't trying to win the war outright. They were baiting us. They wanted him on the field.

He went anyway.

Because strength, to my father, was not just a tactic.

It was a religion.

The battle at the Sable Ridge should have been a slaughter.

On paper, we had the advantage—numbers, terrain, experience.

But paper burns.

I wasn't there when the lines collapsed.

I wasn't there when the Marcerin strike teams—silent, cloaked in frost armor—circled behind our forward units.

I only know what the survivors said later:

That the king fought like winter incarnate. That he shattered spears with his bare hands. That his roar cracked ice at the edges of the ridge.

And that when Lucien himself stepped onto the field, the air grew colder still.

It wasn't a duel.

It wasn't even a fair fight.

Lucien didn't fight for honor.

He fought to end a dynasty.

They say he didn't even draw a sword—just raised a hand, signaling his agents hidden among the Marcerin forces.

A pulse of sonic energy ruptured the ridge face.

The ice broke.

The mountain broke.

King Thalos fell with it.

They found him hours later.

Half-buried under crushed stone and twisted iron.

Still breathing.

Barely.

They brought him back under heavy guard.

Noctis Valerius—prince, soldier, inheritor—stood silent at the gates as the procession returned.

The healers said he was alive.

Said the machines were keeping his heart steady.

Said the old blood of Valerius still clung to life with teeth and broken nails.

But when I looked into his eyes—

I knew he was already gone.

Cersei took control the next morning.

No coronation.

No ceremony.

Just a command whispered down the halls:

"All decisions pass through Cersei Valerius now."

And the nobles obeyed.

Because when the heart of winter falls silent, you listen to the wind that remains.

I stood in the silent hall that night, staring at the empty throne.

And for the first time, I realized:

The throne wasn't empty.

It was waiting.

For me.

Or for the thing I was becoming.

The Witness stirred beneath my skin.

The frost crept higher on the mirrors.

And somewhere far beyond the frozen walls of Erythra, I imagined Lucien smiling.

Because he hadn't killed my father to take the throne.

He had killed him to leave it wide open.

And wide-open doors are invitations.

For gods.

Or monsters.

Or whatever I was becoming.

Chapter 23: The Winter Line Fractures

The war council was small.

Smaller than it should have been.

Cersei sat at the head of the table, sharp and still, her black uniform stripped of ornament. Only the commanders who had survived the last march remained—and they spoke in clipped, tired voices, trying to pretend the world hadn't shifted under their feet.

I stood behind her.

Silent.

Watching.

Listening.

They talked about supply lines, about feint attacks, about the gaps Lucien's forces had exposed. None of it mattered. Not really.

Everyone in that room knew the truth:

House Valerius was bleeding. And no one outside its gates would lift a hand to stop it.

Not for loyalty.

Not for fear.

Not anymore.

The council ended without decisions.

Only orders for more defensive lines. More resource conscription. More pretending.

Cersei dismissed them with a glance.

I waited until the hall cleared before stepping closer.

"You can't hold it together forever," I said.

She didn't look up from the maps.

"I don't have to," she said. "I just have to hold it long enough."

"For what?"

She didn't answer.

Maybe she didn't know.

Maybe she did—and it scared her more than losing.

I left her there.

The halls of the palace twisted beneath my feet, familiar and foreign at once.

I didn't notice the robed figure until he stepped from the shadows near the old frost chapel.

Elias.

He didn't bow.

He only looked at me with eyes that seemed older than the walls.

"The Solariate wishes to speak with you," he said.

Not an invitation.

A summons.

The chapel beneath the palace was older than even the Valerius line.

Built before the first stone of the throne hall.

They led me through side doors, down spiral stairs cut directly into the mountain's bones.

A dozen figures knelt around the frozen altar.

Humming.

Chanting.

Their words weren't in any language spoken in the cities above.

But I understood them.

Because the Witness whispered the translations into my ear as they spoke.

"When the Stone King falls, the Silent Heir shall rise."

"When the crown cracks, the flame shall burn anew."

"Born of ice, born of sorrow, born of silence."

I stood there, frozen, as they finished.

No one looked at me.

They didn't have to.

They were already speaking to me.

Or speaking because of me

Elias approached after the others filed out in silence.

He didn't meet my gaze.

"They believe you are Ith'Kaladrin," he said. "They believe your father's fall was prophecy fulfilled."

"And you?" I asked.

He hesitated.

"I believe prophecy is a mirror," he said finally. "It shows us what we want to see."

"And what do you see?"

He looked tired. So much older than before.

"I see the beginning," he said. "And the end."

That night, back in my quarters, the frost on the mirror shifted again.

This time, there was no doorway.

No invitation.

Only words.

Etched into the cracks.

Words the Witness breathed across the glass like a second skin.

"One will shatter the blade."

"One will shatter the crown."

"One will shatter the flame."

I touched the ice.

It didn't melt beneath my fingers.

It burned.

And somewhere deep inside the shattered halls of my own mind, I felt the cold truth:

It was never about saving the crown.

It was about surviving the fall.

Chapter 24: Before the Quiet Breaks

The frost clung to the windows, thick and stubborn.

It was past midnight, but the light in the war room still burned—soft, sallow, as if the fire itself had grown tired.

I leaned against the far wall, arms crossed, watching Cersei pore over a dozen fractured reports.

Another ambush at the northern outpost. Another rebellion in the mining cities. Another diplomatic envoy that never returned.

The world was fraying, thread by thread.

She didn't look up when she spoke.

"We're not going to survive this, Noctis."

I didn't answer.

She rubbed her temples, a rare crack in her perfect composure. "Even if we win every battle from here forward... the others won't forget how close we came to bleeding out."

"You underestimate fear," I said. "People worship survival."

"Fear fades," she said. "Memory doesn't."

I pushed off the wall and crossed to the table.

The maps were a mess of ink and tears, patches added hastily where entire territories had shifted sides. The old borders of Valerius looked like relics of a civilization that had already fallen.

Cersei placed her hand over the heart of our territory—the mountains of Erythra, the cradle of our power.

She closed her eyes.

For a moment, I saw not the cold commander, but my sister—the girl who once shielded me from court politics with a sword in one hand and a stolen sweet in the other.

But when she opened her eyes, the softness was gone.

Only calculation remained.

"You need to be careful," she said.

"Of what?"

"Of yourself."

I stared at her.

"You think I'm losing control."

"I think..." *She hesitated; the word heavy.* "I think you're starting to believe the things they're saying."

I laughed, low and humorless.

"They're the ones saying it. Not me."

"But you believe it," *she said, voice cutting sharper now.* "I see it in the way you move. In the way you look at the throne when you think no one's watching."

I said nothing.

What could I say?

That she was wrong?

That I didn't feel the Witness breathing deeper inside my chest every time someone whispered Ith'Kaladrin?

That I didn't want to believe I was the answer to everything falling apart?

Cersei stepped around the table and stood directly in front of me.

"You are my brother," *she said.* "I would burn this entire world to keep you alive."

"But if you lose yourself—"

Her voice cracked slightly. Just enough that I knew it cost her.

"I won't follow you into the abyss."

The snow rattled against the windows like a hand trying to claw its way inside.

I looked down at the table.

At the maps.

At the broken lines of old power.

And I realized something Cersei hadn't.

None of it could be shared anymore.

There wasn't room for old alliances. Old loyalties. Not in a world that devoured anything weaker than its coldest king.

I exhaled once. Steady.

Then whispered it—more to myself than her:

"There can only be one. And it's gotta be me."

She heard it.

I knew she did.

But she didn't argue.

She only turned away, the weight of what neither of us could say hanging heavier than the storm outside.

Later, alone in the half-lit corridors, I pressed my hand against the frost-rimmed stone.

The Witness stirred beneath my skin.

And for the first time, I didn't fight it.

Not because I wanted to.

Because there was no other way left.

Chapter 25: The Space Between Silence

The snow was soft against the palace stones.

It fell in thin, whispering veils, blurring the walls, the towers, the world itself into something half-dreamed.

I found her near the eastern watchtower.

Lyra stood alone, her back to me, watching the snow drift down into the black trees beyond the wall. Her armor was half-shed, the shoulder plates lying forgotten at her feet. She looked smaller without them. Almost breakable.

I didn't announce myself.

I just stepped closer, until the cold between us was gone.

She spoke first.

"You shouldn't be here."

"I know."

"You have a war to fight."

"I know," I said again.

The silence stretched — not sharp, not angry. Just... tired. Worn thin by everything neither of us had said before.

"I'm sorry," I said.

This time, she turned.

Her eyes were not soft. Not forgiving. But they weren't hard either. They were the eyes of someone who had been hurt and hadn't decided yet whether to reach out or turn away.

"For what?" she asked.

"For all of it."

The words tasted raw. Unfinished.

"I never meant for this," I said. "I never meant to become—"

"You didn't," she cut me off quietly. "Not all at once."

She studied me for a long moment, as if weighing whether there was still enough left of the boy, she knew to believe in.

"I miss you," she whispered.

"I miss you too."

No walls between us now.

Just the truth.

She stepped forward.

I met her halfway.

The kiss was slow at first — hesitant, as if we were both afraid the other would vanish. Then deeper. Warmer. Her hands tangled in my hair, pulling me closer, and the weight of everything we had lost slipped away for just one moment.

The snow outside melted against the windows.

Inside, only heat.

We didn't rush.

We undressed each other with reverence, not urgency. Each touch was a question answered, a fear soothed. She was real beneath my hands — not a ghost, not a memory. Real.

When we fell into the bed, it wasn't about survival.

It wasn't about forgetting.

It was about holding onto something — someone — while we still could.

Later, as the fire guttered low in the hearth, I traced the line of her spine with the back of my hand.

She stirred, but didn't open her eyes.

"You'll come back," she murmured, not a question, not a command — just a wish, fragile as glass.

"I promise," I said.

A lie, maybe.

But a necessary one.

I held her until she drifted into sleep, her breathing soft against my chest.

I stayed longer than I should have.

I left before sunrise.

Not because I wanted to.

Because the world outside would not wait for love.

The first signs were small.

A broken lock. A trail of frost-burned footprints.

The guards at her quarters found too late. Killed or dragged away.

When they broke down her door, the room was already cold — unnaturally so, as if the heat we had made between us had been ripped away by something worse than winter.

The bed was torn apart.

The walls were scorched.

And carved into the stone above her empty cot, a mark:

A twisted sigil burned in black ice — the sign of those who no longer saw me as a prince, or a savior.

Only as a weapon.

And they had taken from me the only thing left that had ever made me believe I was more than that.

The order came down from Cersei by midmorning:

Suppress the rebellion.

I didn't wait for her permission.

I didn't wait for anyone.

I armed myself and boarded the first skiff heading south.

I wasn't going to suppress anything.

I was going to erase it.

Chapter 26: And I Burned Them Too

The skiff carved through the storm like a blade.

Wind battered the hull, shaking the steel plates, but I didn't flinch. I barely felt it. Every breath I took tasted like iron. Every heartbeat hammered against the chains wrapping tighter around my ribs.

I didn't speak to the soldiers packed in behind me.

They didn't ask for orders.

They knew what this was.

Not a battle.

Not a negotiation.

A reckoning.

The village was smaller than I remembered from the old maps—just a cluster of stone and timber at the base of the southern ridges, nestled between frozen fields.

Smoke rose from several rooftops, but not the kind that spoke of hearths or cooking fires.

The kind that spoke of desecration.

I dismounted before the skiff fully touched down.

Sword drawn.

The snow muffled everything—footsteps, the crack of breaking doors, the shallow gasps of those too terrified to run.

The rebels had made no effort to fortify the village.

Because they didn't expect mercy.

Because they didn't need it.

I found her in the square.

Tied to one of the old Solariate statues—its face half-eroded by centuries of frost.

Lyra.

Her hair, once bright with stubborn defiance, now matted with blood. Her armor stripped away, replaced by a crude tunic soaked through with crimson and ash.

They had carved something into the stone above her:

"False Flame."

A mockery.

A warning.

A victory.

I don't remember moving.

One moment I was standing there, staring up at her broken body.

The next, the village was screaming.

The first man I killed didn't have time to beg.

The second tried to run; I cut him down without slowing.

By the time the soldiers realized they were supposed to follow me, half the square was already slick with blood.

I didn't give orders.

I didn't need to.

I moved through the houses like a winter storm, freezing and breaking everything in my path.

The rebels fought back at first.

Then they just ran.

It didn't matter.

Men.

Women.

Children.

It didn't matter.

I found the ringleader—the one who had led the kidnapping—cowering in a cellar beneath the tavern.

He spat at me when I kicked down the door.

"You're no king," he snarled. "You're a curse."

I lifted him with one hand, slammed him against the frost-cracked wall.

He struggled, gasping.

I leaned in close, so only he could hear me.

"There can only be one."

Then I crushed his throat and let him fall.

By nightfall, the village was gone.

Not surrendered.

Not occupied.

Gone.

We burned it to the bedrock.

Salted the ashes so nothing could grow there again.

The soldiers didn't speak to me afterward.

Some wouldn't meet my eyes.

Others looked at me like they were waiting for permission to turn their swords on themselves.

I didn't care.

I stood alone in the center of the ruins, the snow falling black with ash.

And for the first time, I understood what the Witness had been whispering all along:

It wasn't about building anything.

It was about surviving the destruction.

I looked up at the sky, empty and cold.

And when the wind carried away the last smoke of the dead, I whispered:

"Them too."

The world didn't answer.

Only the frost.

Only the silence.

Only me.

Chapter 27: The Silent Court

The doors of the great hall swung open at my approach.

Not in welcome.

Not in ceremony.

Just necessity.

I walked through the center aisle, past the rows of nobles draped in mourning black, their heads low but their eyes sharp.
Not in sorrow.
In calculation.

Every step echoed.

Every gaze weighed and measured.

I had killed the rebellion.

I had killed everything else too.

Cersei stood at the dais beneath the shattered crest of Valerius.

No throne behind her.

Not yet.

Her expression was a mask carved from the same ice that clung to the windows.

She did not smile.

She did not move to greet me.

She simply watched.

As did the others.

Lord Halric of the Western Marches.

Lady Veyra of the mining colonies.

High Minister Kaelen, his hands trembling just slightly as he clutched the edge of the table.

Loyalists.

Survivors.

And now... doubters.

High Minister Kaelen spoke first.

His voice cracked on the first word but steadied through sheer necessity.

"We have received reports," he said, "of the... outcome in the south."

Noctis Valerius, butcher of Erythra.

I said nothing.

Kaelen swallowed hard.

"The destruction of the settlement was... complete."

Still, I said nothing.

He pressed on, gathering what little courage the old blood could lend him.

"There are questions among the people. Questions among the houses. About proportionality. About judgment."

He didn't say about massacre.

He didn't need to.

The word hung between us like smoke.

Lady Veyra stepped forward.

"If we are to survive, we must control the narrative," she said. Her voice was cooler, sharper.
"Declare Noctis the rightful Ith'Kaladrin. The Coldborn Flame. Let the world see this... purge... as fulfillment of prophecy."

Several heads nodded, slow and uncertain.

Others didn't move at all.

Then Halric spoke.

"Or strip him of command entirely."

The words cracked through the room like a whip.

Silence.

Thick.

Waiting.

Cersei's jaw tightened just slightly.

Only for a moment.

Then she turned her gaze to me.

No accusation.

No pity.

Just... expectation

I met her eyes.

I could see the memory there.

Of a little boy clinging to his sister's hand at their mother's funeral.

Of a boy who once believed the world could be different.

I saw the crack forming.

Small.

But fatal.

I stepped forward, slow and deliberate.

No grand speech.

No defense.

Only a whisper that filled the entire court.

"There can only be one."

A reminder.

A warning.

A truth.

Kaelen flinched.

Halric's hand tightened on the hilt of his ceremonial dagger.

Lady Veyra smiled thinly, the smile of someone who thinks they can ride the storm they've summoned.

Cersei said nothing.

And in that nothing, I heard the future unfolding.

The court session ended without a decree.

No exile.

No coronation.

No absolution.

Just silence.

The kind that comes before an avalanche.

The kind that doesn't need words to promise death.

I left the hall the way I had entered.

Alone.

The frost curling tighter around the cracks in the marble.

The Witness stirred beneath my skin, pleased.

And for the first time, I didn't push it away.

Not because I agreed.

But because it was the only voice left that didn't tremble when it spoke my name.

Chapter 28: Stormlines

The frost never left the windows now.

It webbed across the glass even in the deepest chambers of the palace, creeping like veins of something sick and slow.

I walked the halls in silence.

No one dared approach me.

Not the guards.

Not the ministers.

Not even the acolytes of the Solariate, who once bowed low when I passed.

The halls were wide enough to hold banners and shields and the songs of old victories.

Now they only held cold.

And me.

Elias found me near the outer cloister, where the oldest statues stood buried up to their chests in snowdrifts.

He didn't bow.

He didn't speak right away.

Just stood there, as if the words would break if said too quickly.

"We laid her to rest yesterday," he said quietly.

I said nothing.

"You were missed."

I turned my head slightly, enough to meet his gaze without offering anything more.

"She isn't the one who should be mourning," I said.

And walked on.

Far across the snows, under the shadow of the broken mountains, another storm gathered.

Lucien Marcerin stood atop the ramparts of an occupied Valerius fortress, his cloak snapping in the wind.

The fortress had once belonged to House Iral, a minor vassal loyal to my father.

Now it wore Marcerin colors.

Lucien watched as his forces marshaled below—rows of banners too numerous to count, units trained for cold warfare, siege engines built to crack the very bones of mountain strongholds.

He held a scroll in one hand—sealed not with wax, but with blood.

An ultimatum.

One he would deliver personally.

Behind him, his advisors argued.

Some urged caution.

Others demanded immediate invasion.

Lucien listened.

Smiled.

And decided.

The war would not end with a siege.

It would end with the shattering of a bloodline.

He would break House Valerius not by starving it out—but by ripping its last heir from the stones with his own hands.

Back at Erythra, the council prepared for war.

Cersei gathered what strength we had left—fortifying the cities, consolidating the outposts.

She spoke of logistics, of tactics, of alliances.

She never spoke of me.

And I never offered.

I trained alone.

Sparred against stone dummies until the blades cracked from the cold.

Stared into the frostbitten mirrors until the cracks became veins across my reflection.

The Witness whispered at the edge of my mind.

Soft.

Steady.

I did not resist.

There was no one left to save me.

And I was tired of pretending I wanted to be saved.

The storm lines were drawn.

Not in ink.

Not in treaties.

In blood.

And soon, when the frost broke, the snow would run red enough to bury everything old.

Everything that mattered.

Everything that dared to call itself home.

Chapter 29: Embers in the Snow

The first word came by scout skiff.

An outpost lost.

Not abandoned.

Not surrendered.

Overrun.

I stood with Cersei and the surviving generals on the overlook tower, the wind howling around us like a mourning song. The message was simple, burned into a strip of hide and pinned to the body of the courier who had managed to survive long enough to deliver it:

"Your kings are dead. Your crowns are ash. Yield before the frost devours you."

No signature.

But I knew whose hand wrote it.

Lucien.

Cersei said nothing as she read it.

Only her jaw tightened, the faintest movement, before she handed the scrap back to Kaelen without a word.

The generals muttered among themselves—panic, demands for retaliation, for escalation.

I said nothing.

Because something colder than the snow settled inside me.

This wasn't a declaration of war.

It was a declaration of inevitability.

By nightfall, the sky over the southern horizon burned red—another fortress fallen.

Two more banners lost.

Another thousand dead.

And still no sign of Lucien himself.

Three days later, the invitation came.

Delivered by a messenger in Marcerin colors under a flag of truce.

A meeting.

No armies.

No ambush.

Just words.

Cersei gathered her council in the main hall, debating whether to answer.

Debating whether it was a trap.

I didn't debate.

"I'll go," I said.

Cersei looked at me for a long time.

Measuring.

Calculating.

Finally, she nodded.

"Then end it," she said.

I didn't ask what she meant.

Because it didn't matter.

End it by words.

End it by blade.

It didn't matter anymore.

The meeting place was a ruined chapel on the border of Valerius lands, half-buried in snow.

I arrived first.

Waited in silence.

Watched the clouds roll low and heavy across the horizon.

When Lucien stepped through the broken archway, he wasn't armed.

He didn't need to be.

His words would cut sharper than any blade.

We faced each other across the cracked stone floor, the shattered altar between us.

Lucien smiled—a slow, cold thing.

"I had hoped it wouldn't come to this," he said.

I said nothing.

"You and I," he continued, "we were raised better than this. Raised to build something better."

Still, I said nothing.

Lucien's smile widened slightly.

"You know, when I was a boy, I admired King Thalos," he said. "I thought him unbreakable."

He took a step closer.

"Turns out he was just like every other petty tyrant. A narcissistic coward too blinded by his own reflection to see his house crumbling around him."

Another step.

"And now—"

He stopped barely a pace away.

Looked me in the eyes.

Smiled like a knife sliding between ribs.

"You've done his legacy proud."

Something inside me twisted.

Not rage.

Not grief.

Something quieter.

Colder.

The part of me that remembered holding Lyra in the dark and swearing I'd come back.

The part of me that remembered a sister's hand gripping mine at the edge of the world.

The part of me that knew none of it mattered anymore.

I drew no weapon.

I spoke no challenge.

I only smiled back.

A hollow, empty thing.

"I'll see you at the end, Lucien," I said.

He nodded once, as if sealing a pact.

Then turned and walked away into the snow.

Leaving the chapel—and the last pieces of what I had been—broken behind him.

Back at Erythra, the fires guttered low.

Cersei stood over the maps, tracing the lines of lost territory with a gloved finger.

She didn't look up when I entered.

"The nobles are panicking," she said. "The council is fragmenting. Supplies are collapsing."

Still, she didn't look up.

"The people are dying, Noctis."

Her voice was softer now.

Smaller.

"You can't save them."

I didn't argue.

I only stood there, watching the last threads of a kingdom unravel in her hands.

And somewhere, deep beneath the frost-choked halls of memory, I understood:

The war was already over.

We just hadn't signed the surrender yet.

Chapter 30: When the Frost Breaks

The war council met in secret.

No banners.

No recorders.

No history.

Only silence and snow pressing against the thick stone walls of the inner sanctum.

Cersei stood at the center of the old strategy chamber, surrounded by the few nobles and generals still loyal enough—or desperate enough—to answer her summons.

Their faces were grim.

Their voices low.

Because they knew.

We had lost.

Not in a grand, shattering collapse.

Not in the blaze of glory the songs might have promised.

In attrition.

In cold.

In fear.

The envoy from House Marcerin waited with gloved hands folded neatly at the table's edge.

He wore no armor.

He didn't need it.

Words were sharper now than blades.

"You must understand," he said, his voice smooth as ice, "our lord has no wish for unnecessary bloodshed. Peace can be achieved. An end to the war. A future."

Cersei said nothing.

The envoy smiled.

"But there are... conditions."

The terms were simple.

And cruel.

A marriage.

A union between House Marcerin and House Valerius—to solidify peace.

Cersei.

Lucien.

A crown shared between conqueror and conquered.

The envoy placed a second scroll on the table.

No ceremony.

Just necessity.

"And the prince?" Cersei asked, her voice almost too steady.

The envoy did not hesitate.

"He cannot remain. His presence is... volatile."

A pause.

Measured.

"If he stays, Lord Lucien cannot guarantee his safety."

The meaning beneath the words was clear.

Noctis would not survive the new peace.

Not as a symbol.

Not as a threat.

Not as anything

The room tilted.

Not visibly.

But in the way a dying star tilts the space around it, dragging everything into silence.

Cersei lowered her gaze to the scroll.

She didn't speak.

She didn't move.

Because to speak would be to choose.

And to choose would be to kill her brother—or save him at the cost of everything they had bled for.

Later, after the council had dissolved into frightened whispers and hurried oaths of fealty, Cersei remained alone.

The snow outside thickened into a slow, endless fall.

She stared at the empty map table.

At the crumbling lines of their empire.

At the places where her brother's victories and sins were etched into frost and memory.

She pressed one hand against the cold stone.

Closed her eyes.

And whispered:

"Forgive me."

The decision was made that night.

There would be no announcement.

No ceremony.

Only action.

A truce would be signed.

A marriage would be sealed.

And Noctis—

Noctis would be sent away under cover of diplomatic necessity.

Exiled.

Alive.

Free, if he could find it.

But no longer welcome.

No longer home.

It was the only way to save him.

And the surest way to break him.

The frost thickened against the palace gates.

The first storm had passed.

But the true winter was just beginning.

Chapter 31: Ghosts at the Gate

Something was wrong.

I felt it long before I saw it.

The palace had grown quieter.

Not just from the thinning of soldiers, the fleeing of servants, or the exhaustion clinging to the walls.

It was a different kind of silence.

The kind that came before a betrayal.

Or a funeral.

I stood at the edge of the southern courtyard, staring out over the endless frost fields.

The sky was bruised and heavy with coming snow, but no storm had broken yet.

Only stillness.

Only the faint, shivering cold that wormed under the skin and made everything feel brittle.

Fragile.

Waiting.

Elias found me there.

He didn't approach immediately.

He stood a few paces back, robes pulled tight against the cold, watching me like a man unsure if he was about to speak to a king or a corpse.

Finally, he stepped forward.

"You should be inside," he said.

I didn't answer.

He shifted his weight slightly.

"They're preparing something."

My jaw tightened.

I had known.

Even if no one had spoken it aloud.

Even if no one dared to look me in the eye anymore.

"They think they can save what's left," Elias said softly.

Save.

I almost laughed.

The only thing left to save was a ghost, and ghosts had no place among the living.

I turned to face him fully.

"Who?" I asked.

He hesitated.

Long enough that the answer became obvious.

"Cersei."

The word settled like ash.

Not heavy.

Just final.

The memory of her, standing tall in the council chambers, her voice slicing through fear, her hand gripping mine when I was too young to understand the weight she carried alone—it rose like a knife in my chest.

She wasn't betraying me.

She was saving me.

In the only way left to her.

Even if it meant breaking both of us in the process.

"When?" I asked.

Elias shook his head.

"Soon."

Another pause.

Then, lower:

"You should run."

The old priest's voice cracked on the last word.

"You should leave before they can finish it."

I looked past him, past the walls, past the crumbling banners still hanging limp against the frost.

Run.

Exile myself before they could do it for me.

Disappear into the cold wastes beyond Erythra, where names and bloodlines meant nothing.

Become a ghost in truth, not just in memory.

I closed my eyes.

And for a moment, I almost let myself imagine it.

Freedom.

An end to the whispers.

An end to the war.

An end to everything.

But when I opened my eyes again, the cold hadn't changed.

Neither had I.

I shook my head once.

Slow.

Final.

"If I leave," I said, "they win."

Not Lucien.

Not the nobles.

Not even the Solariate.

The world.

The world that had carved me into a weapon, and now wanted to discard me before I could finish what it started.

Elias bowed his head.

Not in agreement.

Not in defeat.

Just sorrow.

He left without another word.

I stood alone at the edge of the world, the snow beginning to fall in thick, lazy flakes.

It didn't matter if I ran.

It didn't matter if I stayed.

The end was already written.

The only thing left was to choose how loudly I would scream before the silence swallowed me whole.

Chapter 32: Frost Upon the Crow

The great hall was draped in silver and white.

A thousand candles guttered against the frost-heavy air, throwing long shadows across the stone.

It should have been a celebration.

An end to war.

A beginning of peace.

Instead, it felt like a funeral.

I stood at the base of the dais, hands loose at my sides, head unbowed.

The nobles filled the rows behind me, whispering, watching.

No one spoke to me.

No one dared.

Their loyalty had already shifted like ice breaking underfoot—quiet, deadly, inevitable.

At the center of it all stood Cersei.

My sister.

The warborn heir of House Valerius.

Draped in the formal colors of union—silver for mourning, white for surrender.

She looked radiant.

She looked broken.

She didn't look at me.

Not once.

Lucien Marcerin stood beside her, dressed in the muted steel of his house.

He didn't gloat.

He didn't smile.

He didn't need to.

Victory spoke louder than any words.

The High Minister Kaelen, voice shaking slightly, began the proclamations.

"The War of the Frostborn Houses has ended."

"The union of House Valerius and House Marcerin shall bring about a new era of peace."

"The sacrifices made will not be forgotten."

Each word fell like a stone into a frozen lake.

No ripples.

Only cracks.

"And as a final act of reconciliation," Kaelen continued, eyes darting across the assembly, "it is decreed that Prince Noctis Valerius shall take leave of Erythra."

Polite words.

Pretty words.

Exile wrapped in velvet.

A murmur ran through the hall.

Some with relief.

Some with confusion.

A few with shame.

None with courage.

I said nothing.

I didn't move.

I felt the Witness stirring under my skin, an ancient hunger whispering to lash out, to seize, to destroy.

I silenced it.

Not because I agreed.

Because I would not give them the satisfaction.

Kaelen cleared his throat.

"You are granted safe passage from the palace to the outer worlds. No harm shall come to you under the banners of the new alliance."

Safe passage.

Like I was a merchant or a stranger.

Like I hadn't bled for these stones.

Cersei stepped forward.

She unfastened the ring from her right hand—our mother's ring—and set it on the altar between us.

Not handing it to me.

Leaving it there.

A symbol.

An apology.

A farewell.

For a moment, I thought she would say something.

Anything.

But the silence held.

She couldn't break it.

And neither could I.

I crossed the hall slowly.

Each step echoing like a hammer blow against the bones of a kingdom.

I took the ring.

Closed my fingers around it.

Turned without bowing.

Without looking back.

The doors groaned open before me.

Beyond them, the snows waited.

Empty.

Endless.

Unforgiving.

Just like me.

As I stepped into the blinding cold, the last thing I heard was the low, hollow sound of the doors slamming shut behind me.

*And for the first time since I was a child,
I was truly alone.*

Chapter 33: Ash and Silence

The skiff bucked violently against the thin atmosphere.

I gripped the controls tighter, fighting to keep the nose steady as alarms screamed through the cracked cockpit.

A warning light flashed blood-red across the console: CRITICAL SYSTEMS FAILURE.

Another jolt.

Another scream of tearing metal.

Lucien's final gift.

I should've known exile wouldn't be enough for him.

Not when he could wrap a dagger in velvet and call it mercy.

Not when he could end me without ever lifting a blade.

The surface of Ashveil rushed up to meet me—a vast wasteland of blackened ruins and swirling ash, stretching endless in every direction.

I pulled hard on the thrusters, trying to slow the descent.

Another alarm.

Another failure.

The ground hit like a hammer.

The world tore itself apart around me.

Sparks exploded across the cabin.

Something heavy struck my shoulder, spun me sideways.

Pain seared down my arm.

The last thing I saw before everything went black was the cracked viewport—and beyond it, the smothering ash-choked sky.

I don't know how long I drifted.

Minutes.

Hours.

When I came to, the skiff was a broken carcass, half-buried in soot and glassed sand.

The air inside was thick, burning my lungs with every shallow breath.

The filtration systems were dead.

I staggered to what was left of the emergency locker, found a battered breath mask, and forced it over my mouth.

The seals were cracked.

It would have to do.

I stumbled out into the storm.

The ash lashed at me—tiny razors carried on a dead wind.

The sun was nothing but a pale smear behind the blackened clouds.

The ground beneath my boots crunched like brittle bones.

Nothing lived here.

Nothing sane, at least.

Ashveil wasn't just a ruined planet.

It was a graveyard.

A scar.

A warning.

I walked.

Because there was nothing else left to do.

Each step dragged through thick layers of dust and debris.

The ruins loomed around me—shattered towers, gutted bridges, the bones of a once-proud city blackened and hollowed.

The air tasted of rust and old death.

The breath mask filtered little but gave enough to survive another minute. Another hour. No more.

Hours blurred.

Pain blurred.

I didn't know how far I walked.

Didn't know where I was going.

Only that I refused to die here, not yet.

Far above, the ash storms gathered like a living thing.

And far across the stars, a message was delivered to the court of Erythra:

"Prince Noctis Valerius.
Lost in transit.
Presumed dead."

Cersei signed the death notice herself.

Her hand didn't shake.

Her heart did.

But the court never saw it.

Lucien smiled faintly when the news broke.

A smile like someone closing a final ledger.

No witnesses.

No questions.

No threats left alive.

But they were wrong.

I was still breathing.

Still burning.

I collapsed against a broken wall sometime before the second sunset.

My body screamed for rest.

My lungs fought every breath.

Through the cracked lenses of my mask, the ashstorm glowed—deep oranges and reds streaking the black.

Somewhere far beyond reason, beyond exhaustion, I felt the Witness stir.

Whispering.

Not in words.

In hunger.

In promise.

I pressed my back against the stone.

I stared into the dying light.

And I made a new vow.

Not to return.

Not to reclaim.

Not even to survive.

I would endure.

Not for them.

Not for honor.

Not for the memory of a dead house or a broken crown.

For myself.

For the fire that would not die, no matter how deep they buried it.

I closed my eyes.

The ash fell like snow.

And the world turned to silence.

Chapter 34: Broken Crowns and Ash Roads

The days blurred together.

Or maybe they didn't.

Maybe it was just one endless stretch of ash-choked sky, broken ground, and the slow grind of survival.

I moved through the ruins like a ghost.

Hands bloodied from climbing shattered walls.

Feet raw inside cracked boots.

The breath mask kept me alive — barely.
Each inhale felt like dragging knives into my lungs.

The storms never stopped.

Some nights the ash fell so thick it felt like drowning without water.

There was no food.

No water.

Only wreckage.

Only the hollow bones of a world that had died long before I fell into it.

I scavenged what I could — rusted canisters, shattered solar panels, strips of synthetic cloth.

Pathetic trophies.

But they bought me another hour.

Another step.

Another breath.

The Witness whispered sometimes.

Not words.

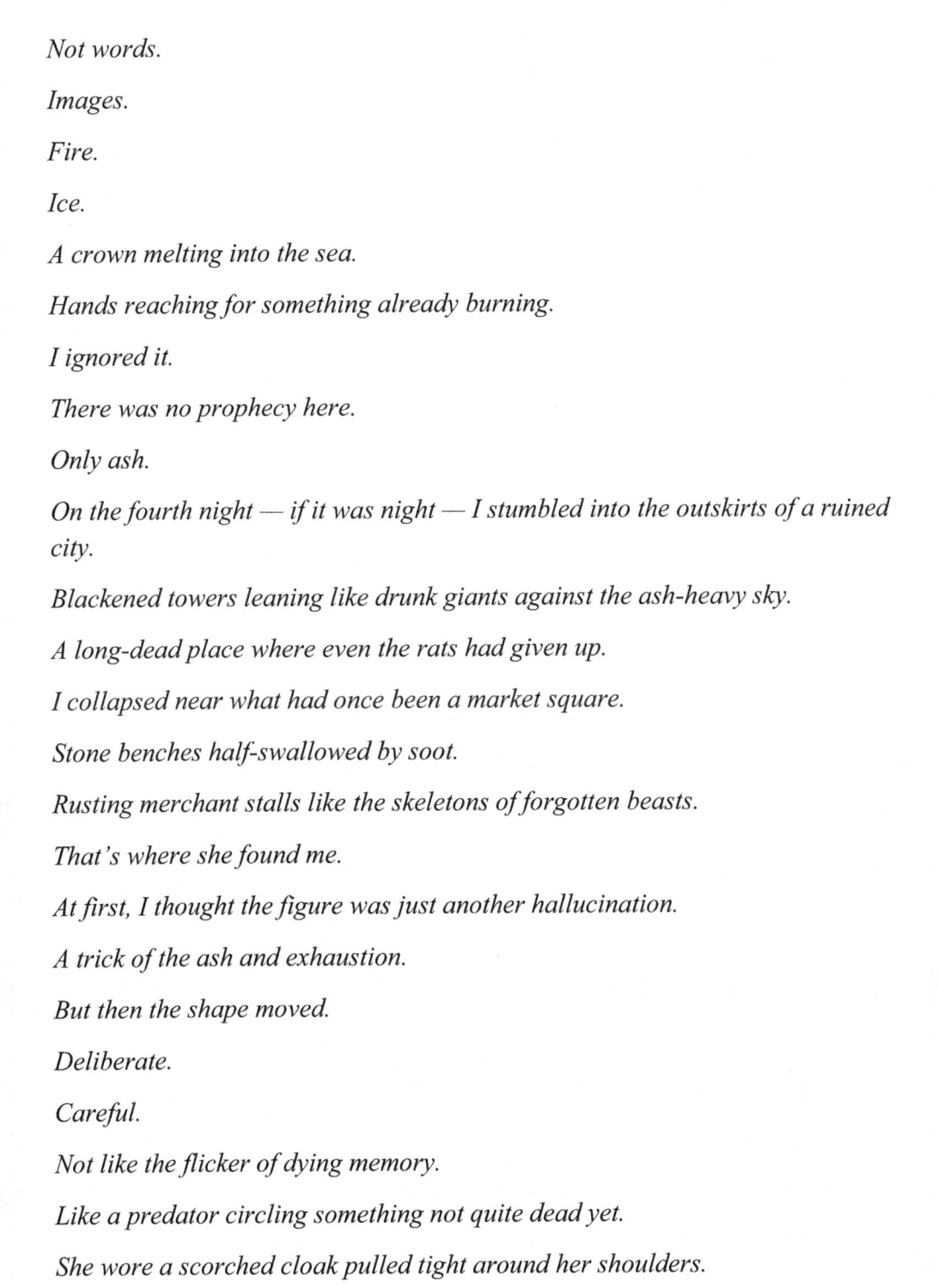

Images.

Fire.

Ice.

A crown melting into the sea.

Hands reaching for something already burning.

I ignored it.

There was no prophecy here.

Only ash.

On the fourth night — if it was night — I stumbled into the outskirts of a ruined city.

Blackened towers leaning like drunk giants against the ash-heavy sky.

A long-dead place where even the rats had given up.

I collapsed near what had once been a market square.

Stone benches half-swallowed by soot.

Rusting merchant stalls like the skeletons of forgotten beasts.

That's where she found me.

At first, I thought the figure was just another hallucination.

A trick of the ash and exhaustion.

But then the shape moved.

Deliberate.

Careful.

Not like the flicker of dying memory.

Like a predator circling something not quite dead yet.

She wore a scorched cloak pulled tight around her shoulders.

A battered breath mask hid the lower half of her face, but her eyes were sharp, clear, cutting through the storm.

She carried herself like someone who had learned long ago that trust was more dangerous than hunger.

She watched me for a long moment.

Silent.

Measuring.

Then she knelt, yanked the cracked breath mask from my face, and shoved a newer one into my hands.

"You're either stubborn," she said, voice muffled through her mask, "or stupid."

Her voice was low, flat, almost bored.

The kind of voice that had seen enough death to be unimpressed by another corpse.

I didn't answer.

Didn't have the strength.

I fitted the new mask over my face, coughing weakly into the filter.

The air tasted like old metal and burning.

Better than nothing.

The woman stood.

Tilted her head slightly, studying me like she hadn't quite decided whether I was salvageable.

"You'll die if you stay here."

Another beat.

"Maybe that's the point."

She turned, starting to walk away.

The ash swirled around her, swallowing her shape.

For a moment, I considered letting her go.

Letting the ruins take me.

Letting the fire inside gutter out quietly.

But something deeper stirred — not the Witness, not pride, not even anger.

Something older.

Meaner.

The same thing that had dragged me out of the wreckage.

I pushed myself upright, staggering after her.

Each step a small rebellion.

Each breath a victory.

She heard the crunch of my boots behind her and didn't turn around.

But she didn't leave, either.

We walked into the dying city together.

Not as companions.

Not yet.

Only as two things the world hadn't managed to kill.

Yet.

Chapter 35: Ash and Hunger

The ruins stretched endless before us.

Dead cities swallowed by black sand and scorched stone.

The sun was little more than a pale smear behind the thick ash clouds, throwing everything into a dull, bloody haze.

We didn't speak much.

Serin moved like a ghost through the wreckage—silent, sharp-eyed, every step measured for survival.

I followed.

Because there was nothing else left to do.

Because stopping meant dying.

The breath mask clung tight against my face, filtering just enough poisoned air to keep me on my feet.

Each breath burned.

Each step dragged.

My body was a litany of aches and old wounds.

My mind—

My mind was worse.

"You should have died with the skiff," the voice said.

Cold.

Amused.

Like someone watching a broken clock tick its last.

I didn't answer.

Didn't even flinch

"But no. Even the world itself can't scrape you out. How disappointing."

The Witness.

Not a whisper anymore.

Not a feeling or a flicker of heat at the back of my mind.

Words.

Clear.

Sharp.

Digging their claws into the bleeding edges of my thoughts.

We picked through the ruins of an old cathedral as the ashstorm thickened around us.

Serin scavenged in silence—rifling through broken crates, shattered prayer stones, anything that might hold food or clean water.

I leaned against a crumbling pillar, fighting to keep my legs from buckling.

"Look at you," the Witness said.
"A prince without a crown. A weapon without a hand to wield it."

"Beg her. Crawl after her scraps. Maybe she'll let you die slower."

I ground my teeth behind the mask.

Shut my eyes.

Willed the voice into silence.

It didn't obey.

Of course it didn't.

It never would.

Serin tossed me a ration pack without looking.

I caught it awkwardly.

Tore it open.

The food inside tasted like chemical dust and regret.

It didn't matter.

It was fuel.

And I needed fuel.

"Good," the Witness purred.
"Feed the fire. Starve the weakness."

The storm outside howled like a dying thing.

The cathedral shuddered under the weight of the wind.

Somewhere beyond the broken walls, I could feel the world shifting — the survivors of Ashveil clinging to life like barnacles on a sinking ship.

This wasn't a place for kings.

This wasn't a place for heroes.

This was a place for monsters.

And survivors.

Sometimes they were the same thing.

Serin sat across the broken hall from me, cleaning a battered blade with a strip of cloth.

She didn't ask my name.

I didn't offer it.

Names were currency here.

And trust was suicide.

"She will leave you," the Witness whispered.
"Or she will kill you. They always do, in the end."

"Better to cut her throat first. Save yourself the ache."

I swallowed the rising anger.

Not because it was wrong.

Because it was too easy.

Too tempting.

Serin finished cleaning her blade and slid it back into its sheath.

She looked at me for a long moment—eyes unreadable behind the scratched lenses of her mask.

"You'll need better gear if you want to survive here," *she said flatly.*

Her voice wasn't cruel.

Just factual.

Like commenting on the weather.

"Stay close tomorrow. If you fall behind, I won't drag you."

I nodded once.

Small.

Sharp.

And in that moment, something unspoken passed between us.

Not trust.

Not friendship.

An understanding.

Two broken things, surviving because they were too stubborn to do anything else.

The Witness chuckled low in the back of my mind.

"Good. Learn. Bleed. Burn. Become what they fear, little prince."

"There's nothing else left for you now."

I didn't answer.

I just sat in the ashes of a dead faith, clutching a cracked ration pack in bleeding fingers, and waited for morning.

If it came.

Chapter 36: The Eyes That Burn

The ruins thinned as we moved east.

Less wreckage.

More silence.

The ashstorms still roared above, but the ground grew harder, the ruins older.

Places where the world had broken cleanly instead of being gnawed apart piece by piece.

Serin led without speaking.

Her strides were steady, sharp, a blade through the choking dust.

I followed.

Breath mask cracked, battered.

Body half-shattered.

But moving.

Always moving

We crested a ridge of blackened stone just as the sun began to melt behind the ash clouds.

Below us, tucked into the bones of a collapsed city, flickered faint lights.

Not fires.

Lanterns.

Weak but stubborn.

Survivors.

Serin muttered something under her breath — almost a prayer, almost a curse.

"They're alive," she said.
"Didn't think anyone stayed this far out.

We made our way down.

Slow.

Careful.

No sudden movements here.

Ashveil's survivors trusted nothing.

No one.

At the edge of the settlement, figures emerged from the gloom.

Cloaked.

Masked.

Weapons half-raised.

Silent as the grave.

One figure stepped forward.

Taller than the others.

Steady.

Unshaking.

Her cloak was stitched from scraps of old royal banners, faded to gray and black.

Her breath mask was old but clean.

Her eyes—
Sharp.
Dark.
Unblinking.

She studied me.

Not Serin.

Me.

Like she was seeing something only she recognized.

Then she spoke.

Voice calm.

Certain.

"You have the eyes of fire."

The others shifted uneasily.

I said nothing.

The Witness whispered in my mind, amused.

"Ah," it said.
"They see it. They see you for what you could be."

The woman stepped closer.

Pulled her mask down.

Dark skin weathered by years of ash and survival.

She spoke again; voice low but clear enough that the gathered survivors heard every word.

"The Coldborn Flame walks among us."

A ripple of murmurs.

Half fear.

Half awe.

Serin stiffened beside me.

Her hand twitched near her blade — not drawing, but close.

I stared at the woman.

Ivara.

I didn't know her name yet.

But I knew the type.

The type who still believed in ghosts.

"You're wrong," I rasped through the filter.

The words felt brittle.

Weak.

Even to my own ears.

Ivara smiled faintly.

Not unkind.

Not mocking.

Just... certain.

"The dead don't walk," she said.
"And yet here you stand."

She turned slightly, addressing the others.

"The Coldborn Flame has returned."

The old prophecy.

The one even I barely remembered.

The one Cersei had whispered over my cradle when I was too young to understand the weight of it.

Serin glanced sideways at me.

Her eyes narrowed slightly behind her cracked lenses.

Not anger.

Not suspicion.

Something colder.

Something closer to fear.

And the Witness laughed inside my mind.

Soft.

Hungry.

"Let them believe," it purred.
"Let them kneel. You will need an army, little prince. And armies are built on belief before they are built on blood."

I closed my eyes for half a heartbeat.

When I opened them, Ivara was still there.

Waiting.

The ashstorm roared above us.

The ruins moaned.

The night fell like a shroud.

And the world tilted around me.

I wasn't a prince anymore.

I wasn't a ghost.

I wasn't even human.

Not in their eyes.

Not anymore.

I was the Coldborn Flame.

And the fire had only just begun to burn.

Chapter 37: Ash Binds the Broken

The camp wasn't much.

A scattering of shattered buildings half-buried in ash and grit.

Torn banners stitched into makeshift walls.

Cracked solar panels barely holding enough charge to power a few flickering lamps.

But it was alive.

And that made it rarer than gold on Ashveil.

Serin and Ivara led me through the outskirts, where the battered survivors huddled around scraps of warmth.

They stared openly.

Not just at me.

At the way I moved.

At the breath mask cracked and patched with blackened tape.

At the eyes they couldn't quite see under the lenses—but sensed anyway.

Ashveil had a language older than words.

It spoke in scars.

In silence.

In who bowed their head and who dared to meet your gaze.

I didn't bow.

And they didn't meet my gaze.

Not yet.

We were given a small ruin near the camp's edge — once a schoolhouse, judging by the crumbling murals and rusted playground wreckage half-swallowed by the dunes.

The roof was half gone.

The air inside tasted less of ash, but more of old death.

It didn't matter.

It was shelter.

And shelter was survival.

Serin dropped a battered satchel onto the cracked floor and leaned against the doorframe.

"You'll need to pull your weight," she said.

Her voice wasn't cold.

It wasn't warm, either.

Just factual.

Like a woman stating the weather report.

"You want to stay? Hunt. Scavenge. Fight when needed. No crown. No titles."

I nodded once.

Slow.

Final.

That version of me had already died in the ruins.

The prince was ashes now.

Only the fire remained.

At night, the ashstorms howled like wolves against the broken walls.

I sat by a guttering firepit, a cracked ration brick in one hand, the other resting loosely near my salvaged blade.

Serin cleaned her weapons with the same steady, methodical focus she always had.

Ivara sat nearby, humming low prayers under her breath—old Solariate songs twisted into survival hymns.

"You should seize this place," the Witness whispered.

"They are weak. Afraid. They would follow strength. They always do."

I ignored it.

For now.

The days bled together

Hunting runs.

Water rationing.

Fighting off wild ash-beasts that prowled the ruins.

Each day the camp watched me.

Measured me.

Whispered about me.

Some whispered hope.

Some whispered fear.

Both would serve, if needed.

Ivara spread the old legends quietly.

No fiery speeches.

No banners.

Just careful seeds, planted in ash and watered with hunger.

"The Coldborn Flame has returned."

"They buried him, but the ashes could not hold him."

"He will forge a path through the wasteland."

I didn't correct her.

I didn't confirm it, either.

Let them believe what they needed.

Serin watched all of it with that same cold, assessing gaze.

Not angry.

Not concerned.

Curious.

Like watching a storm build on the horizon.

The tension grew thicker by the day.

Some of the old camp leaders didn't like how quickly the survivors' loyalties shifted — even subtle shifts.

They didn't like how people watched me when I passed.

Or how they stopped listening quite so eagerly to old orders.

Varek was the loudest among them.

A man built like a broken pillar — broad-shouldered, scarred, with a voice that could shake loose the dust from the rafters.

I first saw him during a ration dispute.

He barked orders, kicked over a water crate, shoved a younger man against the stone with casual violence.

A leader by fear, not by merit.

Ashveil had too many like him.

He saw me watching.

I didn't flinch.

Neither did he.

"That one will come for you soon," the Witness purred in my mind.

"He feels the storm building around you. He thinks he can break it before it breaks him."

Good.

Let him try.

Night fell heavy across the camp.

The fires guttered low against the creeping cold.

I sat alone near the crumbled courtyard, sharpening my blade with slow, steady strokes.

The stone sang softly against the metal.

A heartbeat.

A warning.

Footsteps crunched through the ash.

Serin approached, her breath mask dangling from one gloved hand.

She crouched beside me, gaze sharp.

"You know he's going to challenge you, right?"

I didn't stop sharpening.

"Let him."

Serin's mouth twitched — almost a smile.

Not mockery.

Approval.

"You win," she said, "they'll follow you without question."

"And if I lose?"

"You won't."

Simple as that.

The wind howled over the broken walls.

The ashes stirred.

And somewhere beyond the battered ruins, I could feel the world shifting.

The fire growing.

The Coldborn Flame awakening.

Not with a roar.

Not with a speech.

With a blade.

And blood.

Chapter 38: The Fire Beneath the Ash

The camp woke to screams.

Not from nightmares.

Not from hunger.

Real screams.

The kind born of blood and broken bones.

I was already moving before my mind fully caught up.

The blade was in my hand, the breath mask strapped tight over my face, boots slamming against cracked stone as I sprinted toward the noise.

Serin passed me on the left, blade drawn, eyes sharp.

Ivara stayed behind — guarding the children, the wounded.

She knew her role.

Ashveil was never silent.

The storms never slept.

But this—
This was different.

The air crackled with heat and violence.

We crested the main square just as the first raiders crashed through the perimeter—half-mad scavengers wrapped in blood-streaked cloaks; faces hidden behind crude metal masks.

Desperate.

Starving.

Dangerous.

Serin didn't hesitate.

She drove her blade into the first one that charged, ripping it free in a spray of black-red blood.

I moved with her.

Not for glory.

Not for rage.

For survival.

For the fire that refused to die.

The Witness stirred under my skin.

Hungry.

Eager.

"Let me show you how small they are," it whispered.

"Let me show you how little they matter."

I gritted my teeth and fought on my own.

For now.

One of the raiders lunged, swinging a rusted chain.

I sidestepped, grabbed the weapon mid-swing, yanked him off balance, and buried my blade in his side.

Another came at me—a girl no older than sixteen, eyes wide and hollow.

She didn't hesitate.

Neither did I.

A quick slash.

A brutal end.

The courtyard turned red under the ashfall.

The survivors rallied—spurred by Serin's brutal efficiency, by my refusal to fall.

They pushed the raiders back, driving them into the shattered ruins beyond the outer barricades.

When it was over, the camp stood panting, bloodied but alive.

Ash clung to everything—turning the dead and the living alike into statues of dust and sorrow.

I stood in the center of it all, breathing hard, blade dripping.

The survivors watched me.

Not with fear.

Not yet.

With something older.

Older than hate.

Older than loyalty.

Faith.

"See how easily they bend," the Witness purred.

"See how eagerly they cling to you. You could be so much more if you stopped pretending to be less."

I forced the voice down again.

Buried it under the pounding of my heart.

Serin approached, flicking blood from her blade.

She didn't smile.

She didn't congratulate.

She just nodded once.

Sharp.

Precise.

Approval.

Ivara emerged from the rubble, leading a handful of dazed survivors.

Her eyes caught mine.

And she bowed her head—not deeply, not theatrically.

Just enough.

Enough for the others to see.

Enough to light the first real flame.

That night, as the fires burned low and the storm clawed at the broken walls, the survivors whispered around their guttering camps.

Whispered about the Coldborn Flame.

About the red-eyed ghost who fought like a man who had already died once and refused to die again.

Varek watched it all.

Silent.

Seething.

And I knew—

He would not let this stand.

The challenge was coming.

And with it, a choice I could no longer avoid.

Chapter 39: Ash Draws Blood

The challenge came at dawn.

Not with ceremony.

Not with banners.

Just Varek's voice, booming across the ruined courtyard like a hammer against brittle stone.

"I call for Trial."

The camp stilled.

Voices fell silent.

Tools dropped.

Even the ashstorm seemed to hush, waiting.

Trial.

An ancient word.

Older than the cities that crumbled here.

Older than the banners we used to bleed for.

A word that meant one thing on Ashveil: Life or death by combat.

I stood slowly from where I'd been sharpening my blade by the firepit.

Serin didn't say anything.

She didn't need to.

Her hand brushed the hilt of her weapon once—reflexively, like a mother reaching for a child's hand—and then fell away.

This wasn't her fight.

It was mine.

Varek stood at the center of the courtyard, ash swirling around him.

No armor.

No tricks.

Just a blade longer than my forearm strapped to his back and a face carved from rage and hunger.

The survivors gathered.

Huddled along the broken walls and shattered archways.

Some wore hope like a badge.

Some wore fear like a shield.

Most wore nothing at all — too broken for dreams anymore.

I walked toward him.

Slow.

Measured.

The weight of a hundred eyes on my back.

The breath mask hissed softly with each poisoned inhale.

The ash crunched beneath my boots.

Varek grinned when I stopped a few paces away.

"You're no flame," he said.

Voice rough.

Raw.

"You're just another liar. Another parasite feeding on the last scraps of a dead world."

His hand went to the hilt of his blade.

Slow.

Obvious.

Invitation or threat — didn't matter.

"You want this world?" he said.
"You want these people?"

He spat into the dust.

"Take them."

High above, the ashstorm rumbled.

Not thunder.

Just the earth remembering how to break.

"Kill him," the Witness whispered.

"Show them strength. Show them what crawled out of the ruins when kings died."

I said nothing.

No speeches.

No threats.

I drew my blade in a single slow, deliberate motion.

The metal caught the weak light filtering through the ash clouds.

Not shining.

Not bright.

Just cold.

Ready.

Varek grunted approval.

And the duel began.

There were no rules.

No boundaries.

Only the ash and the blood.

Varek came at me fast — heavier than I expected, but not slow.

A brutal overhead swing aimed to split my skull.

I sidestepped — barely — feeling the rush of air as the blade missed by inches.

Countered with a quick slash toward his side.

He twisted, the edge grazing armor instead of flesh.

The camp pressed closer.

Silent.

Watching.

Breathless.

Varek pressed harder.

Heavy, crushing blows.

No finesse.

Just raw strength.

Every impact rattled my bones.

Every block sent shocks up my arms.

"You are wasting yourself," the Witness whispered.

"Take it. Let me in. Let me end this."

Another swing.

Another crash of steel.

I fought the voice.

Fought Varek.

Fought the part of myself that wanted to give in — to end this with a snap of power

But I was tiring.

Varek wasn't.

And the camp was watching.

Waiting.

Needing

Another blow drove me to one knee.

Ash bit into the wounds on my hands and arms, stinging like acid.

My blade felt heavy.

My breath rattled in my chest.

Varek raised his sword for the killing blow.

And the Witness spoke, soft and sure:

"You will die here. Forgotten. Unless you take what is yours."

*"You are the Coldborn Flame.
You were never meant to burn quietly."*

I closed my eyes for half a heartbeat.

And opened the door.

Just a crack.

The power surged through me — cold and bright and endless.

My body moved faster than thought.

I dodged the killing blow by a hairsbreadth.

Slashed up under Varek's guard.

Felt the blade bite flesh.

He staggered.

Blood sprayed across the ash.

Not enough.

I lunged — blade flashing — and drove it through his chest in a single, brutal thrust.

Varek gasped.

Choked.

Fell.

The courtyard was silent.

Even the wind seemed to bow.

I stood over him, chest heaving.

The Witness whispered in my mind:

"Good."

"Now they are yours.

I looked up.

The survivors stared back.

Some with awe.

Some with terror.

All with recognition.

Serin watched from the edge of the crowd.

She didn't look horrified.

She didn't flinch.

She just nodded once.

Sharp.

Proud.

Ivara knelt.

A slow, deliberate motion.

A prayer.

A coronation.

I pulled my blade free from Varek's corpse.

The ash swallowed the blood before it could stain the earth.

And I stood tall in the ruins of the world that had forgotten me.

Noctis Valerius was dead.

Only the Coldborn Flame remained.

Chapter 40: The Coldborn Flame

The ash buried Varek before the sun had even risen.

No graves here.

No markers.

Ashveil swallowed the dead and left no memory behind.

I stood at the center of the courtyard as the survivors dispersed.

Some drifted away in silence.

Others knelt briefly before disappearing into the ruins.

None dared meet my gaze for long.

None dared challenge what they had seen.

Serin stayed close.

Silent.

Sharp-eyed.

A ghost at my side.

Not out of fear.

Not out of pity.

Out of recognition.

I had crossed a line in blood and ash.

And there was no crossing back.

Ivara approached as the storm thickened above.

She pulled down her breath mask, revealing a face streaked with soot and something close to reverence.

"You have walked through the fire," she said softly, voice low enough only I could hear.
"And you have not been consumed."

She knelt again.

Not to the prince I once was.

To the Coldborn Flame I had become.

The survivors followed suit.

One by one.

Some out of faith.

Some out of fear.

Most out of something between.

I said nothing.

No grand speeches.

No proclamations.

Words were cheap on Ashveil.

Ashveil respected only strength.

Only survival.

Only the fire that refused to die.

"You see now," the Witness murmured in the hollow of my mind.
"You were never meant to crawl. Never meant to kneel."

"You are the flame that burns what the old world left behind."

I should have been disgusted.

Should have rejected the voice.

The power.

The way my hands had moved faster, sharper during the fight — not entirely my own.

But I didn't.

Not fully.

Because part of me agreed.

Part of me knew that the boy who once feared his own strength was dead in the ruins with Varek.

What remained was something harder.

Sharper.

Necessary.

Night fell heavy across the ruins.

I stood watch at the broken edge of the camp, the wind hurling ash against my cloak.

Far beyond the mountains, lightning rippled against the black clouds.

A storm building.

Bigger than anything we had seen before.

Serin came to stand beside me, cloak wrapped tight against the cold.

For a long time, we said nothing.

Only the storm spoke — low and hungry across the shattered horizon.

"You did what you had to," Serin said finally.

Not as comfort.

Not as judgment.

Just a fact.

As immutable as the ash under our boots.

I nodded once.

No words.

She glanced sideways at me.

*"I don't follow kings," she said.
"I follow storms."*

A pause.

"And I think you're going to be the worst one they've ever seen."

Then she turned and vanished back into the ruins.

I stayed where I was.

Breathing the poisoned air through cracked filters.

Feeling the Witness stir — not as a foreign thing now, but as a part of me.

A buried ember.

Waiting for more fuel.

Waiting to burn brighter.

In the ruins behind me, the survivors rebuilt their camp around a new name.

A new banner.

The Coldborn Flame.

Not Noctis Valerius.

Not anymore.

The ashstorm screamed overhead, tearing at the dead city with invisible claws.

And somewhere deep inside, I screamed with it.

Chapter 41: Ashveil's Silent Oath

Ashveil didn't celebrate victories.

It endured them

In the days after the duel, the camp shifted around me in ways too quiet for speeches, too heavy for songs.

The wounded survivors gathered their dead in silence and buried them in shallow graves beyond the perimeter.

The healthy rebuilt walls, scavenged for supplies, reforged old weapons.

And every set of eyes—
every torn, battered soul—
turned to me without asking.

Without demanding.

Simply waiting.

Waiting to see if the Coldborn Flame would rise or flicker out.

Waiting to see if the fire was real.

I gathered them at dusk.

No banners.

No thrones.

Just the broken courtyard where the ash still bore the stains of Varek's blood.

Serin stood beside me.

Not as a bodyguard.

Not as a counselor.

Simply as a sword.

Ready.

Ivara stood too, her cloak stirring faintly in the poisoned wind, her breath mask slung low around her neck.

Her hands were clasped before her, a quiet symbol of faith that spoke louder than words.

The survivors formed a wide ring around me.

Men, women, children.

Ash-streaked faces.

Eyes hollow from years of starvation, war, and worse.

But still alive.

Still watching.

Still hoping.

I said nothing for a long time.

Let the silence press against them.

Let the ashstorms scream above without drowning me out.

Let the world hear itself break.

Finally, I spoke.

Low.

Steady.

Without ceremony.

"You know what I am."

The wind tugged at my cloak, swirling black dust around my boots.

"You know what I am not."

Some flinched.

Some straightened their spines.

Some bowed their heads.

"I am not your king," I said.

"I am not your god."

I looked across their faces—scarred, scared, stubborn.

"I am the fire they tried to smother.
The storm they tried to cage.
The blade they thought lost in the dark."

The breath mask hissed at my side as I inhaled the poisoned air.

The witness stirred at the edge of my thoughts, coiling like smoke.

"If you follow me," I said, voice sharpening, "you follow ash and ruin.
You follow blood and bone.
You follow fire."

A few survivors—ones who had been closest to Varek—shifted uncomfortably.

One stepped forward.

An older man with a ruined arm wrapped in faded red cloth.

He knelt.

No words.

No oaths.

Just the simple weight of survival bending before something stronger.

Others followed.

Slowly.

One by one.

Bowing heads.

Kneeling in the ash.

Ivara knelt last.

She spoke softly.

Just loud enough for the circle to hear:

"The Coldborn Flame will light the path through the wasteland.
It will burn away the old sins.
And from the ashes, a new dawn will rise."

The survivors echoed the last line.

Not all.

Not many.

But enough.

Enough for the first seeds to take root.

Serin didn't kneel.

She simply stood a step behind me, hand resting lightly on the hilt of her sword, her gaze steady.

Loyalty not out of worship.

Out of respect.

The ashstorm howled overhead.

The fires guttered low.

And in the ruins of a world that had long since forgotten how to hope, something new was born.

Not a kingdom.

Not yet.

Not an empire.

Not yet

Only a silent oath.

Bound in ash.

Forged in blood.

Lit by a flame that refused to die.

Chapter 42: The Black Storm

The wind shifted at sunset.

We all felt it.

A low, guttural rumble in the bones of the earth.

*The ashstorms were constant here, but this —
this was something older.*

Something worse.

The survivors huddled inside what ruins they could find, tying down tents with fraying rope, patching walls with scavenged scrap.

The younger ones hid in the deeper tunnels.

The elders muttered prayers in the old tongues.

Even the seasoned fighters wore their weapons loosely, not for battle, but for death.

I stood atop the cracked remnants of a collapsed tower, watching the horizon turn black.

Ash peeled off the mountains like smoke bleeding from broken veins.

Lightning flashed deep within the clouds, not white or gold — but red, like veins pulsing across a dying sky

Serin climbed up beside me, breath mask pulled tight against the growing toxic air.

"Never seen it this bad," she said.

Her voice was flat.

Professional.

But her hand rested lightly on her blade.

*"They call it the Black Storm," she added.
"Once every few years. Most camps don't survive."*

I didn't respond.

The fire inside my blood burned hotter as the storm grew closer, gnawing at the edges of my mind.

The Witness stirred, laughing softly in the hollow between my heartbeats.

"Let it come," it whispered.
"Those who survive the fire will be worthy."

I clenched my fists until the cracked skin along my knuckles bled.

I didn't need the Witness to survive this.

I needed will.

I needed the people behind me.

I turned away from the coming storm and climbed down into the courtyard where the survivors waited.

Ash clung to their cloaks.

Their masks.

Their skin.

Their souls.

"We ride this out together," I said, voice carrying across the broken stones. "No one's left behind."

Not a roar.

Not a cry of faith.

Just nods.

A shifting of weight.

The language of Ashveil:
survive or die.

Hours blurred into chaos.

The storm slammed into the camp like a hammer wrapped in knives.

Ash filled the air so thick we had to lash ourselves to broken pillars to avoid being torn away.

Tents shredded into ribbons.

Solar panels shattered like brittle glass.

The weaker walls collapsed under the pressure of screaming wind and rain that stung like acid.

Some of the outer ruins caught fire, fueled by the chemical toxins buried in the soil.

The world burned.

The world drowned.

The world died.

I led rescue runs through the blinding storm, pulling screaming survivors from crumbling towers, digging through ash drifts taller than men.

Serin worked beside me — tireless, silent.

Ivara stayed with the wounded, chanting prayers that vanished into the wind.

I carried a child no older than ten across half the camp after a support beam caved in.

My breath mask cracked in two places.

The ash cut into my mouth and lungs.

But I didn't stop.

"You could save them all," the Witness murmured sweetly.
"Just a little more.
Just open the door wider."

I gritted my teeth and pushed harder.

By dawn, the storm broke.

The camp was half-ruined.

We lost twenty-seven.

Three dozen more wounded.

Supplies smashed.

Shelters gone.

Hope battered but still flickering.

I stood in the rubble, blood dripping from a dozen cuts, lungs burning, muscles shaking.

And I realized something—

They weren't looking at me with desperation anymore.

They were looking at me like I was the only thing left holding the sky together.

Serin slumped against a wall, breathing heavily through her mask.

"You kept them alive," she rasped.

Not a compliment.

Not a judgment.

Just a fact.

Ivara approached as the ash settled.

"You fulfilled the third sign," she said quietly, voice trembling with awe. "The Coldborn Flame endures the storm the earth itself cannot."

I didn't answer.

I couldn't.

Later that evening, as we rebuilt what little we could, a battered trader staggered into camp.

An outsider.

Filthy.

Bleeding.

Carrying nothing but rumors and old news.

Around a guttering fire, he spoke between coughs.

Spoke of the Empire consolidating power.

Of new banners rising.

Of old heroes falling.

And he spoke, too, of whispers:

"They say," he croaked, "one of the Winter Blades lives still.
A woman.
Refused to kneel when the new regime crowned itself.
Disappeared into the wastes, carrying a blade they tried to break."

I froze.

Something in my chest twisted.

Serin watched me carefully but said nothing.

The trader shrugged.

"Could be a lie. Could be nothing.
Ashveil eats hope faster than corpses."

He spat into the fire and wrapped his cloak tighter.

But the ember was lit.

Commander Ysra.

Maybe dead.

Maybe alive.

Maybe a ghost.

I stared into the flames long after the others drifted to sleep.

The storm outside had passed.

But another one had just begun inside me.

Chapter 43: Embers Beneath the Ruins

Ash still drifted from the broken sky.

Not in great storms anymore.

Not in violent rivers.

Just a slow, endless rain.

As if the world itself was bleeding out by degrees.

We rebuilt what we could.

Stone by stone.

Scrap by scrap.

Not because it would last.

But because it had to.

The survivors moved differently now.

Quieter.

More efficient.

When I spoke, they listened.

When I ordered, they obeyed.

Not with the wide-eyed desperation of the first weeks.

Not even with the wary loyalty earned after Varek's death.

This was something else.

Something heavier.

A silent agreement.

We are ash.

We are flame.

We are what endures when everything else breaks.

Serin stood by my side as I oversaw the rebuilding of the northern walls—her breath mask pulled down, eyes scanning every movement with the cold precision of a soldier at war.

She spoke little these days.

She didn't need to.

At night, we gathered by the cracked remains of the old cathedral, huddled near the embers of salvaged fires.

The wounded slept in its broken shadow.

The children played in its hollow bones.

The future—the ugly, stubborn future—grew there in the ruins.

It was on one of those nights that Ivara spoke.

Not to the crowd.

Not to stir them.

Just to me.

She sat across the fire, her hands folded loosely in her lap, the flickering flames painting shadows across her soot-streaked skin.

"You know what you are to them," she said.

Not a question.

I didn't respond.

Didn't need to.

"You are the Coldborn Flame," she continued.
"The third sign has come—the Ashveil Wound, the Storm of Black Breath, the Blood in the Ruins."

I looked at her.

Really looked.

Saw not the quiet acolyte she pretended to be.

Saw the fierce, burning certainty behind her calm face.

She wasn't hoping I was Ith'Kaladrin.

She had decided I was.

And nothing—not storms, not blood, not even death—would shake her belief.

"The old prophecies said the Flame would suffer," she said.
"That he would be broken.
That he would be remade."

She met my gaze across the fire.

Unafraid.

Unwavering.

"And when the Fourth Sign comes," she said, voice low and sure, "the world will know it can no longer be ruled by old kings."

The Fourth Sign.

I didn't ask what it was.

Didn't want to know.

The Witness stirred in the back of my mind.

Not mocking.

Not laughing.

Simply watching.

Patient.

Waiting.

Later, after the camp settled into uneasy sleep, I walked the ruins alone.

Past the collapsed walls.

Past the graves marked with nothing but broken stones.

The stars above were faint through the drifting ash.

But they were there.

Distant.

Uncaring.

Beautiful in a way that made my chest ache.

I thought of Commander Ysra.

Of a broken blade, somewhere beyond these ruined skies, refusing to kneel.

Of a world that had left me for dead and now dared to whisper my name in hope again.

And I thought of the Fourth Sign.

Of what price it might demand.

"You already know," the Witness whispered in the hollow of my heart. "It demands you."

I closed my eyes.

Felt the ash on my skin.

Felt the slow, endless hunger burning in my blood.

And I understood:

The boy who had dreamed of escape was dead.

The prince who had believed in loyalty was dead.

Even the man who fought for survival was dying.

Only the fire remained.

Chapter 44: Fire Cannot Be Caged

They tried to run in the night.

Twelve of them.

Armed, desperate, and quiet.

But not quiet enough.

Serin caught the first one near the north barricade, boot pressed to his throat, a half-packed satchel of stolen rations still clutched in shaking hands. He begged. She didn't strike him, didn't need to. She just looked at him.

I watched the others as they were dragged into the courtyard. Half of them were scared. The rest were angry. One was crying.

"We were just going to leave," one of the older men said. "We weren't going to hurt anyone."

"You already did," Serin said flatly, tossing the stolen water canister at his feet. It cracked open against the stone, bleeding its contents into the dust.

I didn't raise my voice. Didn't call for trial. There was no trial for betrayal here.

"You were going to take the supplies meant for the children," I said. "You would have let them starve so you could crawl away into the dark."

"It's not crawling if the fire's going to burn us all," someone muttered.

I stepped toward him. He backed away, fast, as if my very presence might ignite him.

"We fought for this," I said. "We bled for this. And now you want to run with full packs while the rest carry nothing but wounds?"

"We didn't ask for this flame. We didn't ask for a prophet."

"No," I said. "You didn't. But you lived because of me."

The fire inside me stirred. Not the Witness—me. My anger. My resolve. My understanding.

I looked across the faces of the camp. They had gathered in silence, in the same place where Varek once stood. No one stepped forward to defend the deserters.

"We can't afford doubt," I said. "Not now. Not after everything."

One of them tried to bolt.

Serin moved like a blade loosed from its sheath. Two steps. A flash of steel.

He collapsed mid-sprint, throat open. No one screamed. Not even him.

The others froze.

I looked them over, then gave the slightest nod.

Serin and two other loyal survivors moved. The executions were fast. Brutal. Efficient.

It wasn't justice.

It was necessity.

When it was over, the courtyard was quiet again. The only sound was the wind tugging at the broken walls.

I turned to the rest of the survivors.

"If anyone else wants to leave, do it now. But you walk with nothing."

No one moved.

Good.

I left the bodies where they fell. Let the ash take them.

That night, I stood at the edge of the watchtower. Serin joined me eventually, silent as always.

"You're not the boy I met," she said.

"No. I'm not."

"You're better," she said.

I didn't answer.

I stared out over the horizon, where the ash drifted like ghosts. Somewhere out there, the old world still waited, smug and untouched.

But the fire here was real.

And it was mine.

Chapter 45: The Weight of a Crown

I climbed the ruins of the cathedral alone.

The wind cut harder up here, slicing through the cracks in my cloak, carrying the ash like snow. The black kind. The kind that never melts, only settles deeper.

Beneath me, the camp moved with slow, steady rhythm—fires flickering in makeshift braziers, voices low, movement minimal. We had survived another day. They had survived because I refused to let them die.

I sat at the edge of the broken stone balcony. The stars above were pale and thin through the clouds, but they were there. Watching. Distant. Unbothered.

The air was quiet except for the wind and the faint whistle of ash scraping past ruined stone.

I didn't feel proud. I didn't feel powerful.

I felt hollow.

Like the fire inside me burned so hot, it had eaten everything else.

A month ago, I was a prince. A reluctant one. Hiding in marble halls while my sister wore steel and duty like armor. A name. A weight.

Now, no one called me Noctis Valerius.

Now, I was something else.

Below, I could see Ivara praying near the fires, her voice soft, hands moving in strange, practiced gestures. Around her, a few survivors sat cross-legged, heads bowed. She was already teaching them something. A faith. A way.

They didn't follow a man.

They followed the Coldborn Flame.

And I wasn't sure I still knew the difference.

The Witness stirred.

It didn't speak. Not this time.

It just sat in the quiet with me.

And maybe that was worse.

Because it felt natural.

It felt right.

It felt like it belonged there.

I thought of Cersei. Of Erythra. Of Lyra.

Of Ysra, maybe still alive, maybe not.

Of the snow.

Of the way it used to fall—cold, clean, soft.

Not like this ash that coated everything in grief.

I didn't cry. I hadn't in weeks. Maybe months.

But I let the cold press into me. I let the stillness settle around my bones. I let the last pieces of the boy I was crumble into the wind.

The wind didn't care.

The world didn't care.

Only the fire remained.

And for now, that was enough.